W9-AXG-474

PRAISE FOR BESTSELLING AUTHOR JUDITH GUEST'S NOVEL
THE TARNISHED EYE

"*The Tarnished Eye* is wonderful, written in spare prose that achieves a swift pace and a compelling elegance of tone and mood. The characters are so real that their insistence on hope, in the face of inexplicable evil, suggests how all of us might best cope in these perilous times."

—Dean Koontz

"Judith Guest's superb style is only part of why you'll want to read *The Tarnished Eye*. Beautifully written, it also supplies both high-wire suspense and characters with a finely drawn trueness. You'll come away with a sense of knowing these people, the places they inhabit, and the power of their secrets. Haunting and unforgettable."

—Jan Burke, Edgar-winning author of *Bones, Eighteen,* and *Bloodlines*

"A superb novel. The biggest showcase this book offers is the author's mastery with character development. Judith Guest is a terrific writer and she has proved it time and time again. *The Tarnished Eye* is no exception, it is the real thing."

—*I Love a Mystery* newsletter

"*Ordinary People* and *Errands* were such powerful stories about family relationships, grief, and the inner workings of the human mind and heart, I was curious what Guest would do with the mindset of a murderer. Guest does not disappoint her readers. Packed with suspense. . . ."

—*Women's Lifestyle*

" 'This is a sweetheart of a novel, a real sweetheart,' as the late writer Andrew Debeus used to say about the books he really admired. . . . Though there is [a] terrible murder at the heart of things, there's still something wonderful on every page, things you won't want to miss."

—*All Things Considered,* National Public Radio

"Judith Guest brings new depth and emotion to the police procedural with this finely woven tale of family, death, duty, and redemption."

—Pete Hautman, author of *Mrs. Million*

"The gathering momentum is irresistible. By maintaining the plot's welcome and even necessary swiftness while at the same time tending to character development, depth, and differentiation, Guest produces a novel shivering with artistry and darkness."

—*Booklist,* starred review

"Loosely based on an actual unsolved crime that occurred in Michigan in the late 1960s, this tightly paced, gripping thriller is imbued with substance, sensitivity, and depth. A finely tuned page-turner."

—*Publishers Weekly*

"In a classy domestic whodunit, a backwoods sheriff tracks the killer of a troubled Michigan family. Brisk and highly readable; Guest has a keen eye for the delicate fault lines that underlie family life and excels at showing us the ravages of domestic collapse."

—*Kirkus Reviews*

"In *The Tarnished Eye*, Judith Guest has crafted a poignant and suspenseful novel that gives full weight to the victims. A well-drawn country sheriff tries to maintain a balance between the personal and the professional while hunting for their killer, but it is the victims themselves who emerge on the page rounded and whole and heartbreakingly human."

—Margaret Maron, Edgar-winning author of *Last Lessons of Summer*

"A rich, powerful novel of how crime bleeds from the dead to the living, haunting even the most gentle of moments. Judith Guest's portrayal of northern Michigan's beauty torn asunder reminds us all to lock our doors at night."

—R. D. Zimmerman, author of *Innuendo*

ALSO BY JUDITH GUEST

Errands

Killing Time in St. Cloud
(with Rebecca Hill)

Second Heaven

Ordinary People

JUDITH GUEST

THE TARNISHED EYE

Pocket Star Books

New York   London   Toronto   Sydney

The sale of this book without its cover is unauthorized. If you purchased this book without a cover, you should be aware that it was reported to the publisher as "unsold and destroyed." Neither the author nor the publisher has received payment for the sale of this "stripped book."

 A Pocket Star Book published by
POCKET BOOKS, a division of Simon & Schuster, Inc.
1230 Avenue of the Americas, New York, NY 10020

This book is a work of fiction. Names, characters, places and incidents are products of the author's imagination or are used fictitiously. Any resemblance to actual events or locales or persons, living or dead, is entirely coincidental.

Copyright © 2004 by Judith Guest

Originally published in hardcover in 2004 by Scribner

All rights reserved, including the right to reproduce this book or portions thereof in any form whatsoever. For information address Scribner, 1230 Avenue of the Americas, New York, NY 10020

ISBN-13: 978-1-4516-1330-8

This Pocket Star Books paperback edition January 2006

10   9   8   7   6   5   4   3   2   1

POCKET STAR BOOKS and colophon are registered trademarks of Simon & Schuster, Inc.

Cover design by Tom McKeveny
Cover photo © Bob Stefko/Veer

Manufactured in the United States of America

For information about special discounts for bulk purchases, please contact Simon & Schuster Special Sales at 1-800-456-6798 or business@simonandschuster.com.

To my husband, Larry
And to my grandchildren:
Andre, Priya, Jesse, Harry,
Olivia, Isabel, and Lauren

Acknowledgments

The idea for this novel was originally inspired by a crime that occurred in Michigan in the late 1960s. To date, that crime remains unsolved. I wish to thank the Women of Pilford Pines, who first urged me to write this story. I also wish to thank Alcona County Sheriff Doug Ellinger for his help on all matters of police procedure. Thanks, also, to Tom Ware for his attention to detail, and to my son, Larry, whose careful reading and inspired suggestions enabled the book to finally come together for me. I am so grateful to all of you.

Harrisville, Michigan
September 28, 2003

He had by nature
a tarnishing eye
that cast discolouration . . .

—*Diana of the Crossways*
George Meredith

THE
TARNISHED
EYE

DIGGING UP

Hugh DeWitt stands at the window, looking out at his wife as she gently uproots slips of lettuce from the soil. She likes pulling the tender new shoots first, leaving room for the rest to grow and prosper. Her garden gloves lie discarded in the middle of the row. Hugh has bought her several pair over the years—these last ones, expensive kidskin from Gardeners' Eden—but she doesn't like them any better than the cheap, cotton variety she picks up at Okum's; they're all too bulky for the job. She needs to get her bare hands

around the slender stems. He loves this para-
dox—his tidy wife, so firm about purity and
order, with this passion for grubbing around in
the dirt.

She's wearing blue knit shorts and a sleeveless
yellow T-shirt. Her feet are bare. Bare knees
pressed into the soft earth. Beside her is the straw
basket Becky made for her in art class, nearly full
of greens. Soon she'll stop, come inside, rinse the
leaves in the sink, and pat them dry between
paper towels.

Beside him, curled up in the wing chair, is his
daughter, busily writing in the pages of her daily
journal. Her grandma Hannah gave her the book
last Christmas, and she hasn't missed a day in the
last seven months. "This is exactly the age when I
started," Hannah told Hugh. "I've been doing it
ever since." When he asked her if she ever went
back to read over the entries, she laughed. "Oh
heavens, no. It's all I can do to just get the stuff
down." What's the point, then, in all this scribbling
if there's no corresponding passion for review,
Hugh wonders. Somehow it doesn't seem polite to
ask.

Becky smiles up at him. "Daddy, d'you know
what a *pluot* is?"

"A pluot," Hugh says, "is nothing. It's a made-
up word."

"It's half plum and half apricot." She shows

him the picture she has drawn, below which she has lettered:

PLUOT

"Mom and I picked some up at Glen's today. They taste like a very firm peach."

"Why don't they just call them peaches, then?"

Becky ignores him. "I was thinking we could make some pluot jam and sell it at a roadside stand. Like the Millers. We could sell green beans and lettuce and heirloom tomatoes out of Mom's garden."

"The Millers," Hugh points out, "are megafarmers. They do this for a living. Plant, weed, water, harvest. Break your back. Get up at five in the morning, go to bed at midnight. And they don't make any money."

"How do you know?"

"Because. Mr. Miller told me. They're thinking about selling the place and moving to the Upper Peninsula."

"Can we buy it, then? Mom loves to garden. She knows tons about fruits and vegetables."

"Your mom knows tons about many things— watercolors, beekeeping, jewelry making, chair caning—"

"She'd make a great farmer," Becky says.

Hugh shakes his head. "Truck farming's not for sissies."

"Who says I'm a sissy?" Karen says, coming in from the kitchen. "Are the Millers really going to sell, Hugh? The twins will graduate next year. I thought they'd be taking over."

Hugh shrugs. "Maybe the twins saw the light."

"Don't say, 'saw the light,'" Karen says. "Farmers going out of business isn't a good thing."

"I didn't say it was. But growing up where everyone knows you and knows what your father does for a living and then assumes it's what you'll do might not be so great either. What if one of them meets somebody at college who isn't so thrilled about becoming a farmer's wife?"

"Is that what happened?"

"I'm merely speculating," says Hugh. "Anyway, Miller says it's getting too crowded down here. He likes the wide-open spaces."

She frowns. "Well, he'll find plenty of space in the U.P., that's for sure—along with rocky land and a shorter growing season."

"I'll tell him you said so."

"When I grow up," Becky says, "I'm going to be a cop."

Not the first time he's heard this threat. "Good. Be a cop. Be a house painter. Dig to China. I'm all for people doing just what they want to in life."

His daughter isn't fooled; she eyes him reprovingly. "Jesse Spence's father says most dads *want* their kids to follow in their footsteps."

"Jesse Spence's dad's a funeral director. He's got to believe that."

Hugh follows Karen into the kitchen, watching as she dumps the lettuce into the sink and turns on the cold water.

"Mom, Dad doesn't believe there's such a thing as a pluot," Becky calls from the living room.

"He didn't use to believe in arugula either," Karen says. "He'll come around."

"It's the corruption," Hugh says. "All this combining of perfectly adequate foodstuffs just to prove that it can be done. I remember once I had a banorange. It tasted terrible." He reaches into the water to grab up a handful of greens, shakes them gently and drops them onto the square of paper towel spread open on the counter. "Want these torn up?"

"Yes, please."

Becky comes to stand in the doorway. "So can we buy the Miller place?"

"No, we cannot," Hugh says. "Law enforcement officers catch criminals and solve crimes and return stolen goods to their rightful owners. They aren't good at growing things."

"Bigger pieces, Dad," Becky advises, moving in

to help. "No need to make confetti out of it." Only ten years old and already she's an expert at bossing him around. "Remember," she says, "Mom and I won't be home for dinner tomorrow. We're going to Traverse City to get me a new swimsuit and some jodhpurs. For camp."

"Ah, yes. Horse camp," Hugh says. "The great money pit. Gotta keep up with that little clothes pony, Donna Merle."

Becky rolls her eyes. "Oh, Daddy," she sighs. "Why do you always have to be such a *daddy?*"

"Light the grill, will you?" Karen asks him. "I was going to cook inside, but it's just too hot."

He carries the plate of cleaned trout out to the backyard. She's right about the heat. Each morning for the past three weeks he has ridden into town with the patrol car windows down and the air-conditioning blasting. By 8 A.M. it feels like a smelting oven; there's been no rain in a month. Fire warnings are at the highest postings. People are starting to call in with all sorts of weird complaints. His deputy, Ian Porterfield, calls it Combustion Craziness.

But that isn't what's bothering him, is it? On this blistering July afternoon? *Three years ago today. Becky at day camp, thank God. An all-day outing in the Sleeping Bear Dunes, an accident of timing. Too bad there are so many of those. Fuck all,* he thinks, *fuck if I'm going to goddamn do this thing all over again.* But he is, obviously.

He reaches below the grill for the lever on the propane tank, gives it a vicious twist. Karen is watching from the window, and he sends her a cheery grin. *Faking it.* They are both faking it today, July the twenty-first, 2004. The third anniversary of their infant son's death. How many years will it take? How many before he can think of it without pain? Without remorse? Before he can simply remember Petey as a pudgy, dark-haired, eleven-month-old, patiently refusing a spoonful of strained peas or pounding his palms on the high chair to gain their attention? Those four tiny ragged teeth; the look of baffled irritation when things didn't go his way; the piercing metrical screams employed to summon them?

Three years ago today Peter Weldman DeWitt simply took it in his head not to wake up from his afternoon nap. *Sudden Infant Death Syndrome,* they called it. No one's fault. An accident of timing. *If you'd happened to enter the nursery at the instant he stopped breathing, you might even have saved him,* the doctor had said. *Fucking wonderful news to drop at a mother's feet.* He was enraged at the stupidity of the remark, enraged at his own stupidity in leaving town that day for a meeting. And he had been driving Karen's car, in order to get it serviced in Ann Arbor. The engine was running rough. Otherwise, he would have been in the patrol car and would have known the instant the call came in, would have turned around, been back in time to go through it with her. Instead, he discovered it on his arrival in Ann Arbor and had to drive the four and a half hours back to Blessed, knowing it was too late, Petey was gone. Gone forever, his feisty, handsome son, who would have been four years old next month. So now there are two calendar dates, forever marked and awkwardly celebrated.

Does Petey's big sister ever think about him? She was so proud of her baby brother, so fiercely protective. Yet she hardly ever mentions his name. But, then, neither does he, and he thinks about him every goddamn day.

At least there is no longer the relentless agony of that first year, nor the awful resignation of the second. He is grateful for the fact that time has passed. And here they are, once again, at this anniversary, which will have to be spoken about; Karen will insist upon it.

She is at the back door now, watching him as he tests the fillets with a fork.

"Just about ready," he says.

"Good." She hesitates in the doorway, and he

knows what's coming, would like to head it off, at least for now.

"You having dinner with your mom tomorrow night? While you're down there?"

"Probably."

"Drive carefully, okay? Call before you start back. Sometimes the cell phone doesn't work along that stretch."

"I will. But don't worry if we're later than ten o'clock." She pulls the door closed behind her. "You know, Hughie, we're not that poor," she says. "A new bathing suit won't break us."

"I know. I'm kidding. She knows I'm kidding."

"Just because your dad was a cop," she says, "doesn't mean you had to become one. You *did* have some choice in the matter."

"I know that. I wasn't saying that."

"What were you saying, then?"

He lifts the fillets, one by one, onto a clean platter. He won't answer this. She knows as well as he does that's not what it's really about.

Hannah, his mother-in-law, is a genius at breaking through to the corner of his mind where Petey still resides, alive and well, dimples flashing, black hair in sweaty ringlets around his face. She, who once gave him a book on the proper way to grieve. He read it, too, but it didn't do much for him. Except now he knows it's wrong to bury this stuff, to refuse to share it with loved ones. And he knows too much—about death and the unexpected, about a world that he took for granted, assuming the forces propelling it were, in the main, orderly and benign. He wouldn't share this knowledge with his worst enemy.

Following Karen into the house, he bows his head briefly, surreptitiously. *Forgive me. Deliver me. Amen.*

EDWARD

THE CABIN SITS at the back of a bluff that is thick with juniper and sweet fern. A stand of crooked jack pine climbs the hillside, gnarled trunks and bent limbs shielding the view of the place from the road. Before he found this piece of land just south of Blessed, with its annex of beach property below, Edward Norbois had already envisioned what it would look like, complete with cabin and outbuildings. Built of huge ponderosa logs imported from California, with a soaring fireplace of river stone. A raised great room, floor-to-ceiling windows, furniture made of cedar and hickory. An ancestral estate. His personal statement: *I'm here, I built this place, I own it.*

He loves the fact that Route 119 is an old logging trail. The jack pines, with their scrawny limbs and rough, twisted trunks, are second- and third-generation trees, and he often wonders what his property might have looked like some two hundred years ago, before the lumber barons arrived. Before men like his great-grandfather Eaton Norbois moved in to transform the landscape.

He, Edward, is a transformer of a different sort; he ordered the excavation, the huge Caterpillar tractors that dug out the switchback leading up to the site, the cement mixers, sand trucks, and log trailers. After them came the roofers, plumbers, electricians, and carpenters— all of it orchestrated by him. He remembers four years ago, when he treated his family to their first view; the walls were barely up, the ridgepole in place. They had gaped in amazement, and then Stephen had said solemnly, "'My name is Ozymandias, king of kings: Look upon my works, ye Mighty, and despair . . .'" and had promptly burst out laughing.

"What's the joke?"

"It's so damn *huge*, Dad."

Still, he hasn't minded inviting his friends up

here for free weekends of food and lodging. Stephen's friends are all alike; loutish-looking football players who slam doors and leave wet bathing suits on chair cushions and forget to pull up the sailboat and the kayak. Edward despises giving up his cherished privacy to types who, had they applied for jobs at his factory, wouldn't have made it past the front door. That blond kid with the earring and the smelly shoes who kept calling him Dude. *Jesus!* And still Stephen complains. He doesn't like spending the summers up here with his brothers and sister, doesn't want to help wash the cars or burn rubbish or haul wood. Maybe he'd rather be going to summer school back in Ann Arbor? Or working for College Craft, painting houses? If he doesn't shape up, he just might find himself doing that.

Edward sluices more water over the top of the BMW, careful not to let the metal end of the hose hit the roof. *Thank God for the trip. I'm ready for it.* He hasn't flown the Cessna in nearly a month. It's waiting for him now, at the airport in Pellston, and he's itching to get his hands on the controls. He filed the flight plan this afternoon and called Anne at work to let her know their schedule. She seemed surprised that they were still planning on it.

"I thought, after your talk this morning with Mr. Frisch—"

He didn't let her finish. "Roger and I have come to an understanding," he told her curtly. Not that it's any of her business. No one comes close to nicking his ego the way Anne does—not even Paige. That's the downside of having had the same secretary for twenty years. She was his right-hand woman when he started Challenge Press, until he hired Roger Frisch and things began to change. Well, now they'd be changing back. But that didn't mean he had to let her in on all the grisly details. Theoretically they'll be out of touch for three weeks; in actual fact, Anne expects him to call in, to be kept apprised of the situation, and to hear about any additional shit that hits the fan.

"You always shoot from the hip," Anne scolded him today. "Then you don't like to face it when things go wrong."

It made Edward wince. Of course Anne had suspected Roger from the first. And then it turned out she was right. But it had all seemed so far-fetched at the time, and he had begun to question her motives, thinking she was trying to turn him against Roger in order to enhance her own position with the company. *Stupid!* Anne is as loyal as family; she'd never do anything that wasn't in the best interest of Challenge Press. He, of all people, should have realized that.

He'd hoped to cut his workweek back this summer to four days; drive up to Blessed on

Thursday and stay until Monday morning. Spend more time with his family. That's out now, of course; he'll be cleaning up this mess of Roger's for the next six months. He hopes that's all he has to sacrifice, hopes he'll be able to make peace with the IRS and that this doesn't evolve into a public fiasco. *Damn Roger anyway!* At least he got the message: pay it back or face criminal charges. No more negotiations. No bullshit about the tax people having made a mistake.

He sponges the car with hard, swift strokes. He likes to leave things in good order while he's away. Tomorrow they'll drive over to Pellston—a half-hour trip at most, it's only seventeen miles—but he wants to get there early enough to pull a tarp over the BMW. They'll leave here at four in the morning so they can take off from the airport by six. Off to Vancouver, Banff, and Lake Louise. He can't wait. The Cessna 206 is a new model for him; he hopes he likes it as well as he did the little Skyhawk.

That'll be something else for Stephen to complain about—leaving at four in the morning. Why does everything have to be so damn *problematical* with him? Hell, he can sleep on the plane. Paige is always so eager to appease him. She'd do almost anything to avoid an argument. Thank God the others aren't as spoiled as his middle son.

Ozymandias. What the hell is that supposed to

mean, anyway? He never did understand that poem. It's the here and now that counts. And life *is* sweet when you have the money and the time to enjoy it.

Of his four kids—Derek, Stephen, David, and Nicole—he finds he is most grateful for his daughter's uncomplicated affection. All of his boys seem to have issues with him; David's timidity and Derek's silent withdrawal are merely two sides of the same coin, and sometimes they are harder to take than Stephen's outright rebellion. He doesn't remember ever having problems like this with his own father; from what he can recall they got along fine. His father would have enjoyed the role of grandfather. Too bad he had died so young.

After he's finished with the car, he'll make sure all of the beach paraphernalia is picked up, the sheds locked, the drapes closed in the living room. Paige is of the opinion that if someone intends to break in, they will do it whether the drapes are open or closed. But Edward has a thing about this, doesn't believe in tempting fate. The television and the VCR, the stereo, the telescope, Nicole's electric piano—all are visible from the windows. What isn't seen won't be coveted.

Early on he decided that putting energy into making friends up here in Blessed would be pointless. He greets people if he sees them on the beach, and that's good enough; having cocktails with them on their front decks is not part of the program. Back in Ann Arbor, socializing with people in the neighborhood has gotten entirely out of hand. Most of them are simply not his type, but because Paige and their next-door neighbor, Elaine Spiteri, have become friends, they now get invited to a lot of boring parties that he would never have chosen to attend.

For the life of him, Edward can't see what Paige sees in Elaine. She's exactly the shallow, rich, country club woman that he abhors. And her husband Matt is a cipher. *Yep, the neighborhood's going to hell,* Stephen said slyly the other day, when he overheard the two of them discussing it over breakfast. Edward is sure it was why Paige blew up at him.

"Elaine likes to do things," Paige was saying. "She's friendly, she's a good golfer, and she likes *me!*"

"Why shouldn't she like *you?* That's not the question, is it?"

"Oh, Edward, you're such a . . . I think you're turning into a *hermit!*" She stormed out of the kitchen, leaving him there, stung. Is she right? Is he a hermit? Just because he's careful about choosing his friends? But then, he's not nearly as careful in business, is he? Not such a great judge of people, as it turns out.

No two ways about it—the talk this morning

with Roger Frisch has taken a lot out of him. He doesn't often spend time second-guessing himself, nor reliving bad moments from the past.

But Edward has always believed in the cooling-off period as an invaluable business tool. The company's assets are safe; its reputation hasn't yet been damaged. If Frisch can find a way out of this with his own character intact, more power to him. Of course this won't satisfy Anne; she would like to see him hung out to dry.

Anne has opinions, and she's not afraid to express them. She has dispensed free advice from the first day he hired her. A single mom whose kids are out of college, she would offer him ideas on how best he should prepare his progeny in the ways of the world. She never did approve of them not working during the summers. Hiking the dunes, sailing the Sunfish, basking and frolicking on their private beach, weren't her notions of how kids should learn to manage money.

"If you make all of their decisions for them, Edward, how will they ever find out how to function in the real world?" she had asked, and he had answered in kind:

"This *is* the real world for my kids, Anne."

She had been shocked for a moment; then slowly her mouth had relaxed into a grin. *Wealth begets wealth. The rich shall inherit the earth.*

He's not worried that his kids will ever have to scrounge and struggle, the way Anne's kids have had to; it just isn't going to happen. And he's not about to start apologizing at this late date for the way he has chosen to live his life.

SLOW THURSDAY

"WILL YOU STOP at Baileys' on the way home tonight?" Karen asks. "Nancy Bailey said she'd lend Becky a sleeping bag for camp."

"When do you leave for camp?" he asks.

Becky, sitting at the kitchen table playing with a dish of fruit, looks up at him.

"Next Sunday." She sighs. "Dad, I told you about a hundred times . . ."

"Well, did you ever think I might be getting senile?"

"No. You just don't listen. You've always been

like that." She pushes the dish of cantaloupe and blueberries away. "Mom, this stuff tastes funny."

"Don't eat it, then. The melon might be too ripe."

"I had some," Hugh says. "I thought it tasted fine."

Becky pushes her chair back. "It's too hot to eat. Let's just get going before the traffic gets bad."

"All right, sweetie." Karen leans over the back of Hugh's chair, kisses him on the cheek. "We're off. Back after dinner."

"Say hi to Hannah for me."

"I will. I left you some cold meat and potato salad. We'll bring you something from the French bakery."

They are out the door and he sits, drinking his coffee, proud of the fact that he didn't tell her, for the fifth time this morning, to drive carefully. He *is* getting better about that. Not that the highway into Traverse City is more dangerous than any of the two-lane roads she travels every day around here. They all have hills and bends, obscured by lush summer greenery. There is no way to protect oneself fully from the unexpected, no guarantees of safety. But there *is* an art to thinking positively. God, would he love to master that one.

He drives the short distance into Blessed, focusing on the glory of the day—no clouds, birds singing, Lake Michigan a ribbon of light in the distance. *Practice optimism. All will be well.*

"Mrs. Clement wants you to come by," Fredda Cousineau says as he enters the office.

"What now?"

"A smell in her woods. She noticed it while she was out on a walk."

"What kind of smell?"

Fredda wrinkles her nose, grinning. "Bad smell. Like something's dead out there."

"Did you suggest that something probably *is* dead out there?"

"I did not." Her grin widens. "I didn't want her telling me to smarten down my mouth, like last time."

"Tried to take it for you, Hugh." Ian Porterfield leans out from behind his cubicle. "She only wants to talk to you. By the way, there's no word yet on the Franklins' truck. Looks like it might be part of some downstate operation."

The chance that Dil Franklin's beat-up Chevrolet has been stolen by anyone other than one of Dil's own goofy relatives is about a million to one, Hugh figures. Maybe it's the long, cold winters that make Ian yearn for excitement. Or maybe he just hasn't lived long enough to cherish the beauty of a day where nothing happens. He's twenty-six years old, three years out of Police Academy, and a restless soul, always at the jump. Hugh was lucky to hire him right out of school. He's a good, solid deputy, and if Hugh doesn't promote him to under sheriff soon, he suspects he could lose him to a town where he has a better chance of moving up.

"Where's Mrs. Clement from, anyway?" Ian asks. "She sounds like a Brit."

"She's from Engadine," Fredda says. "Moved down here when she got married. She's about as British as you are."

Hugh is continually amazed at how much history Fredda knows. The records of everyone in town are at her fingertips; she can rattle off their statistics at will. She is only twenty-two years old; she's been with Hugh since before she graduated from high school. She is the best clerk he's ever had. The scions of her clan—all eight brothers and sisters—traveled down from Canada in the early 1900s to buy up the largely uninhabited territory below the border, along with the oil and mineral rights. As their empire expanded and their many offspring peopled the western shoreline, so their reputation grew as a tribe of unruly and tough Frenchmen. There are few Cousineaus in the area that Fredda is not related to; none that she doesn't know.

"Did you pull the file on the EMS program?"

Hugh asks her. His desk is a mess, as usual. Fredda has offered to clean it up, but he actually prefers it this way.

She hands him the file along with his messages: one from an Officer David Glenn of the Oscoda Police, asking them to be on the lookout for a robbery suspect with relatives in the area; the other from Sarah Clement.

"I typed up your notes from the Forest Service meeting," Fredda says. "Everything's there on top."

"Thanks. Yeah, I see it."

He needs to get to this paperwork. No lunch today; he'll skip it. Getting a little flabby about the middle these days. He noticed it this morning in the mirror.

His glance sweeps across his desk. "You haven't seen my good pen, have you?" He rustles through some papers, and Fredda gets up, crosses over to him, runs her hands expertly under a pile of invoices. She hands him the pen, with a small frown.

"*Honestly,* Boss."

"Thanks."

He can't bring himself to explain how it gives him comfort to live at a certain level of clutter here, in the only place where it's allowed. Fredda probably knows it, anyway, as she is also their baby-sitter. He sometimes worries that, between Karen's hygienic rigidity and his own stoic despair, they will turn their daughter into a scrubbed and tidy depressive. But so far, Becky's nature seems resolutely buoyant.

"You might want to combine your trip to Mrs. Clement's with a stop at Amble-in Antiques," Fredda says. "Ash says somebody tried to jimmy the back door open last night. His dog scared them off. He's not worried, but he thought he ought to report it."

"Now *that* one I will delegate," Hugh says.

"Got it," Ian says from behind the partition.

He pulls in at Sarah Clement's place, and she's waiting for him with cookies and iced tea. He takes a glass of tea but he won't sit down on the worn, horsehair sofa; if he does, he'll be here for a good hour. He's known her nearly all his life, ever since he brought her German shepherd home after the dog was picked up eating out of garbage cans on the shore road.

"Duke knows where he lives," she'd told him tartly. "You tell your daddy to catch some real criminals for a change."

He was twelve years old at the time and bashful as a deer in the presence of any woman besides his mother; he still remembers how she'd looked him over. "I could tell you were a DeWitt. Those big shoulders and blue eyes. You look just like your daddy."

Does he? The picture of his father in the rogues' gallery in the hallway shows him as a tall man with dark hair and boyish features; handsome in an unkempt, rough way. He guesses he does fit that description. But the rebel in him smarts at the comparison: too unimaginative, too pat. Isn't there anything that sets him apart from this revered figure, the only five-term sheriff of Emmet County?

The year he and Karen had returned to Blessed from Detroit, Sarah had made it her personal goal to help get him elected. "Emmet County needs another Sheriff DeWitt," was her slogan. Moving away from a city where positions were plentiful to a town where there was one job and it had to be re-earned every four years was risky. But then, his chances were better than average; his father was a hero in this town.

"What's the problem, Sarah?"

"If you'd come when I first called, you wouldn't have to ask. But now the wind's shifted. It's not so noticeable anymore. Although"—she goes to the door, sniffs the air—"the smell is there, if you know what to look for. Come here," she commands. "Take a good deep breath."

He obeys, even goes out on the porch to lean over the railing, filling his nostrils.

"There. You smell it?"

"I don't notice anything. Just your roses. But we'll check it out for you."

"Don't do it for me, do it for yourselves. Something's dead out there, Hugh. Somebody's shot something out of season, probably. Farmers fed up with deer thieving out of their fields."

"No doubt," he says.

Sarah Clement has lived on the bluff since her parents moved from Engadine. She has a cadre of sons and daughters, most of them still in the area, looking out for her now that her husband Ralph is gone; they buy her groceries and trim out the woods behind her house, keeping things in good order. She doesn't have a car, rarely goes into town anymore, but her mind is as sharp as ever; she knows she's parked on a priceless piece of land, sitting at the very tip of the bluff, coveted by every realtor in town. Someday the place will be inherited by the sons and daughters, but it won't be soon. At seventy-eight, Sarah is the healthiest woman in all of Emmet County.

"Well," he says. "I've got a meeting. I'd better get going."

"How's that cute little girl of yours?" She escorts him down the steps. "What's her name again?"

"Rebecca. She's fine. Getting ready to go to horse camp next week."

"*Horse camp.* Back on my dad's farm, we just climbed up on 'em and rode away. Give my good wishes to your wife, Hugh. She's a fine person. You are one lucky man."

"I am that."

He drinks in the air around Sarah's yard as he heads for his car, smelling only the odor of pine boughs under the heady scent of sweet fern.

Why is it he seems to revert to his twelve-year-old self in her presence? Something about being confronted with the weight of past events—both his and hers. She's had her share of sorrow—losing first her husband and then her oldest son in separate hunting accidents. He's grateful she doesn't mention Petey today; she is one of those people who tends to keep track.

PAIGE

Y ES, I HAVE all that. I'll fax it to the printer right away. And you'll call and check on the table decorations? Great. Thanks, Margaret. You're a gem."

She hangs up the phone with a small sigh. From this moment—five o'clock on the afternoon of June 25—the chairwoman of the Entertainment Committee of the Ann Arbor Day Club is officially on vacation. The banquet will be flawless, and her committee will handle the rest of the details. She gathers up her papers, goes to the fax machine, and dials the printer's number.

One thing she prides herself on: She has great organizational skills. No matter the size of the job or how complicated, she knows how to nail things down. Some people who held this position in the past have tended to micromanage, but she knows how to delegate—from table decorations to seating arrangements to the menu. Paige Norbois knows when to let others take over. It gives her a great sense of satisfaction, even as it scares her to death. Yes, this is her *niche*—party planner. So much for the BA in Education at the University of Michigan.

She is still thinking about this as she scoops shrimp salad into lettuce leaves on individual plates and piles the bread basket full of homemade French rolls. They'll eat on the patio tonight. A perfect summer evening. This is her favorite time of day on the bluff. She loves watching the sky slowly darken from deep coral to the lush violet after the sunset. Tonight the humidity is down and there's a slight breeze blowing. It might keep the mosquitoes away. *Remember to light the citronella candles.* She'd bought them this morning, stopping to make conversation with the young clerk in the store about the coming Fourth of July celebration. She is easing into this small-town life much more quickly than she expected. She could see herself spending even more time up here after the kids are grown. She'd love to turn her garden into a showplace, planting perennials and unusual bulbs and native grasses. She'd invite the old woman who lives up the road over for tea. Sarah Clement, her name is. Nice old lady. But that's a long way into the future. Nikki is only ten and David thirteen. Stephen and Derek will be gone soon, but she still has at least eight or nine child-raising years ahead of her.

She feels a slight twinge of guilt when she thinks of how much she enjoys her privacy up here while Edward is downstate, working. The kids are much looser about the meals; sometimes they don't eat dinner at all, just snack on leftovers and junk food. Some nights she even makes it into bed before dark. She loves lying upstairs in her room, reading, watching the play of leaf and shadow on the walls, listening to her brood arguing amiably over cards downstairs.

It's always a little more peaceful up here when Edward's not around, of course; there's not the tension between him and Stephen. But also, there's a difference in the pace of life. Edward is a doer; he can always think of some household or outdoor tasks that need his and the kids' attention. When he first suggested spending the summer in Blessed, she thought it might mean a relaxation of the activity level that rules their lives back in Ann Arbor. But no; he has managed to drive that same pace up here, including their vacation-within-a-vacation that begins tomorrow morning at 4 A.M.

She gives another long sigh, glancing out the window toward the gravel clearing where her husband is washing his beloved BMW. He spreads water over the top while caressing the roof and sides with a sponge in a slow, regular rhythm. He's wearing his good silk shorts and a clean white T-shirt while he does this. She quells the swift gust of anger rushing through her. Why is he so stubborn? So compulsive? He absolutely *cannot* imagine wearing anything but good clothes, no matter the task, no matter how impractical they may be. *Those shorts cost ninety dollars; they have to be dry-cleaned, for God's sake!*

It is one of the many mysteries of his character. Twenty years of marriage and she is still unable to fathom him. Or to change him, of course. For instance, he will not wait until tomorrow morning to load the car. That will have to be done tonight, so that in the morning their only task will be to get themselves to the airport on time. Which means the kids will have to be all packed, preferably before dinner, so they can have their card games in the living room before they go to bed. Even the leisure activities tend to be performed on schedule when Edward is around.

He's not the sort of guy you can argue with, is he? That is her lover's assessment. Speaking in a slightly mocking tone, but never going too far; always careful not to be disrespectful.

There, now. She has carefully divided the shrimp salad into six equal parts; as usual, it has come out just right. That is another of her skills: an ability to see at a glance how stuff should be apportioned. *An extremely accurate sense of the volume of things, that's what I have.*

Damn. Why this sudden swoop of despair, this heart-stopping fall into utter emptiness? Why does her life suddenly feel like an endless distraction, like *busywork?* Leading her away from herself, away from what she really wants? *Will I ever feel alive again?*

She strikes the kitchen countertop hard enough to bring tears to her eyes. She will not act like a baby, will not lament her fate. Will not perform any of those trite and desperate female rituals resorted to when lust wins out over duty.

The breakup was her idea. She means to stick to it. She refuses to think of him in the present tense. It is over for real this time—no going back. She has kept this promise to herself for nearly three weeks now. She barely thinks of him anymore. Busy with her children, her garden, her clubs, her books. She has a life, after all. She isn't that stupid actress in the play about the couple who've had a secret affair for thirty years and meet once a summer to renew their tired, silly romance.

Turning away from the window she presses her back against the counter. *God, I miss him so much, what's the use of anything?* Misses his gentleness, the boyish sound of his voice over the telephone. His blue, blue eyes; his handsome, sculptured face. Misses the sex. *Oh hell.* The way he likes to grip her fingers lightly between his teeth, moaning softly while she laps at the skin of his stomach, like a big mother cat. Misses his suckling her, as if he were her baby. He's not speedy and fastidious, like Edward. She's not expected to rise immediately, clean herself, and bring a towel for the wet spot. He loves sleeping in the nude, holding her close afterward, stroking her hair, crooning softly in her ear.

Why do things have to be so complicated? Why couldn't she be happy with the situation as it was? "Just learn to live with life's ambiguities," he said in his easygoing and practical way. "Why does this have to be permanent? Why can't we just decide to take a break?" He has always been respectful of her feelings, mindful of her commitments, as he called them. Conveniently, he brought no other relationships to the affair (she always called it by its true name, to keep them honest). But that also made it easier for him—no children, no wife, no calendar to juggle.

What do I really want? She is a thirty-nine-year-old, relatively attractive woman (he says that she is beautiful, but then, he is her lover and expected to sweet-talk and flatter her), married at nineteen and a mother at twenty. And all she can say for herself is that she knows how to play a good game of both golf and tennis and that she gives well-planned parties. Oh, wait: She is also an excellent parallel-parker.

This makes her laugh, and she moves to carry the place mats and silverware out to the patio, arranging them around the wrought-iron table. *Lighten up. It's not the end of the world.* Not yet, at least. Derek is out on a run, Stephen is at the beach. She'll tell Nikki and Davey to go down for a swim before dinner. Then she'll make a couple of martinis and join Edward out in front. She means to talk to him about Stephen. She's not about to go off on a three-week vacation with those two barely speaking. The way they skulk around, avoiding each other, filling the house with tension. They are too much alike, that's the problem. It's unfair to the rest of the family that they insist on taking up all the psychic space.

She grins. Don't use that phrase, though. *Psychic space.* It's exactly the sort of language that drives Edward nuts. He'll put his foot down and refuse to compromise on anything.

Another of the many arcane facts she has gleaned about Edward Norbois over the years. What is marriage after all but a double collection of arcane character traits—both good and bad—thrown together into a peculiar mix? The question is, do they combine well enough to satisfy the two partners over the long haul?

She has made her decision: She *wants* this marriage, wants the safety and predictability of it. And the kids. What would she do without her kids? She will accept what she has and be content, then. *Accept life's ambiguities*. There are all kinds of them, aren't there? You pay your money and you take your choice.

BEFORE THE STORM

FREDDA HANDS HIM a tuna fish sandwich as he walks in.

"I'm skipping lunch today."

"No, you're not," she says. Little Miss Caretaker. "How'd it go with Mrs. Clement?" She hands him his phone messages.

"Fine. I told her it was all in her head."

"You did not."

"It could be anything, with the woods in this condition. I'll send Art and Ollie up there to have a look this afternoon." He glances down at one of the messages. "What's this?"

"She called right after you left. Said her boss was supposed to be back at work a week ago. There's no answer at the family's cabin. She's worried about them. Wants to know if you'd mind checking the place out when you have a chance."

"Now we're responsible for the *turistas* getting back to work on time?" He likes using that word, *turistas;* the same way he likes calling Upper Peninsula natives *"Yoopers."* It makes him feel separate from them in a way that he knows in his heart he is not. "What'd Ian say about the break-in at the antiques store?"

"Some scrapings around the door handle, that's about it. Ian said the lock's so flimsy, anybody could lean against it and it'd fall off. You ever been inside that place?" She shudders. "Who'd want to break down a door and confront that pile of junk?"

"One man's ceiling, Fredda." He pours himself a glass of water from the small sink, drops a couple of ice cubes in it, dumping the rest of the tray into the bowl in the freezer. "I'll be in my office. Eating my tuna fish sandwich and cleaning up my desk."

She grins. "I'll inform the public."

He likes Fredda, likes her toughness and the

nervously proud way she had stood up for herself when she first came to his office looking for a job. Until then he'd known the Cousineau family mainly through her father, René, a dirt farmer and more or less full-time drunk. René had spent a lot of Saturday nights in the Emmet County lockup. His wife Francine had died years ago and the job of raising the four kids had fallen to Fredda. As the oldest sibling, she had done an amazing job of it. Her brother, Eliot, had gotten a scholarship to Michigan State largely through her efforts.

"My dad's pretty much of a souse," she had informed Hugh that first day, "but he isn't a bad person. And I'm a hard worker. I learn fast. I don't think you'll be sorry to have me around." He had hired her on the spot, upgraded her to head clerk when Mary Thornton retired and moved to Florida.

Sitting down at his desk, he clears a small space in front of him. Lunch first; then he'll take care of the phone calls. He shuffles through the slips of pink paper: Officer Glenn from Oscoda again. Rick Fradl wanting to know if they can schedule a meeting with the town commissioners over the wetlands issue. *That sounds like fun.* The secretary from Ann Arbor. Anne Ransome is her name. He gives the slips a prominent place—on top of the phone—so they won't get lost in the shuffle.

Ian opens the door and sticks his head inside: "Got a minute, Hugh?"

"Sure."

"Remember those statues that got stolen from the guy up in Herzl? He called to report the value is over a thousand dollars, which, according to the law, makes it a felony."

"Where'd he get that factoid? On *The Shield*?"

"Says they weigh about a ton apiece. Says he wants to prosecute."

Hugh sighs. "If they ever show up again. Who'd want 'em, anyway? Does he have any ideas on that?"

Ian grins. "I think he's got a pretty good idea who'd want 'em."

"Yeah, that's what it sounds like to me. Okay, maybe they'll settle it among themselves. That'd be a break."

Stolen statues and vanishing wetlands. This is what the job has come down to. Maybe it's just the heat that's getting to him. He'd love to take off to the Au Sable, spend the afternoon fishing with Mack Gellar, debating the merits of fishing streamers or fishing dry, of caddis fly nymph versus Roberts drake. He feels as if he's in a sauna right now, wonders if it's this hot in Colorado, where his brother, Kenny, lives. He should call Kenny one of these days. See how the kids are, how Sally's doing.

Fredda pops her head inside the door: "Want a Coke?"

"Sure."

She crosses the room to his desk, hands the can over to him.

"You ever think about getting a new job?" he asks.

"Nope," she says cheerfully.

He remembers now that he's seen Fredda several times this summer at Coffee Talk with one of the Miller twins. He wonders if they've ever discussed truck farming as a way of life. It doesn't seem like her style, but who can tell? Love could carry her off at any moment.

"Good," he says. "I'm glad."

Without Fredda he'd never know where anything was in this office. It would be a disaster if she were to decide to pick up and move to the U.P.

She gives him a sunny smile. "Try to relax," she advises. "You'll feel better after it rains."

DEREK

AT THE EDGE of the lake the sky is a gorgeous
shade of vermilion; thin threads of coral bleed
through the bank of clouds as the sun plunges
toward the water. If he had his pocket paints he'd
stop and do a quick sketch. He thought about
bringing them, and then changed his mind; he's
on a serious run, getting in shape. And he doesn't
feel like painting, not after last night. *Why does he
save his choicest comments for the dinner table?*
Having to witness everyone's discomfort—Nikki
and his mother, both of them tense on the edges

of their chairs; Davey's faraway look; that sarcastic grin of Steve's, masking his own helplessness. *You're the man, you show us how it's done.* His siblings each have their own troubles with his father; hasn't he seen plenty of this, at countless other meals? Usually you're just happy not to be the one on the hook. As for his mother, he's not sure what her true position is on this issue; he's never really trusted her unconditional acceptance. Does she think he should transfer into art school? He really can't stay in bus ad another semester; he'll lose his mind.

It has to be his decision. He has promised himself not to let either praise or blame affect his view. And, after all, what does his father know about art? Or his mother, for that matter? And they know even less about the people who make it. What would his dad think, for instance, about Jamie Wyeth never finishing high school? He'd think it was nuts. He'd think Wyeth's parents had a screw loose, letting him get away with that. No matter that his father was already a famous painter. High school, college, graduate school: these are the logical steps to take toward a solid future.

All that he himself learned in high school was that life is boring with other people telling you what to do. And, so far, college isn't doing much more. It hasn't gotten him an inch closer to his goal. But it has made one thing clear: business school is out. Forever. He can't go this route. And last night was *it,* as far as putting up with any more wisecracks about artists and their lack of a work ethic. Time to get tough. Ignore all belittling behavior. It's the only way to win with Dad. *He doesn't know everything.* And what he doesn't know about his own kids is enough to fill a goddamn book.

So what was his first thought this morning? That he'd go to Banff without any art supplies, not even a damned charcoal pencil. *Oh, that's brilliant, that'll show everyone, won't it?*

Resolutely he jogs along the footpath that leads back to the cabin. Rounding a curve, he shifts his weight, feels an answering chafing along his right heel—the beginning of a blister. On that one issue Dad is right; too much lying around renders you lazy and out of shape. The feeling in his gut, though—that, sooner or later, his father wins out on every subject—has to be countered by some practical and definitive move on his part. And there is the very real dilemma of how to make a living doing the thing he loves best.

His grandma Pearl should be his guide: She was a wonderful watercolorist, and, despite the fact that she never sold a single painting, she kept the faith. She also never allowed her only son to boss her around. She had a talent for disengaging herself from his powerful perspective with nothing but a smile. She was the only person who could best his father in an argument, coming out of it as serene as when she went in.

He remembers the year before Grandma Pearl died, he did a portrait of her that she loved; she had a wonderfully expressive face—strong and stern, with her inner self blazing through on the paper. He entered the portrait in a juried show and won second prize. After which, he'd given the portrait to his father for Christmas. It hangs in his office. What kind of mixed message is that? *Son, I am so proud of your work. Now, get a real job.*

His grandmother and his father argued many times over her coming to live with them. "I'm serious, Mother. I can't stand the idea of you being sick and alone in that apartment." Pearl just laughed. "I'm neither sick nor alone. And if I were to move in with all of you, the first thing that would happen is I'd become this rickety old thing, running around losing my glasses." His father finally gave up trying to convince her. He remembers how it amazed him that the man could actually be beaten. And at his own game. His father simply didn't listen to other people's opinions when it wasn't in his best interests. He knew what he wanted, and that's what counted. The whole thing was being able to separate *your* needs from *his;* you had to know where you left off and he began.

If he could have stayed in the apartment at school, it would have made things easier. But that was impossible. Not after what happened with Camilla. So he needs to learn how to keep to his own path, despite the pressure he'll get when he tells them of his decision to switch schools. As for his moving out, it had to be done. He couldn't stay there any longer, feeling as he does. The scene with the picture. Hell, it's probably nothing. But he's not sure, needs to think about it. Anyway, it can wait—it'll all have to wait until they get back from Banff.

He stops by a patch of sweet fern to tie his shoelace and a line from a poem rockets through his head: "Art is long, and Time is fleeting." Who said that? Somebody from the nineteenth century, his lazy brain tells him. Something he learned in high school—praise be!—that struck him as meaningful at the time. How does the rest of it go?

Funeral marches. He straightens to a standing position, pushing for the rest of it, but it's not there.

Ask Davey. Davey knows all manner of screwy things, is smart in the way of memory work, like a computer. Amazing what's logged into that twerpy thirteen-year-old brain—literature, history, politics, science, geography, sports trivia; he can spew it out at a moment's notice. Dad calls him the Renaissance Man.

Art is long, and Time is fleeting,
  And our hearts, though stout and brave,
Still, like muffled drums, are beating
  Funeral marches to the grave. . . .

Creepy little poem. *A Psalm of Life,* by Henry Wadsworth Longfellow. So it seems that he did occasionally listen, back in high school. Good for him!

He rounds the corner of the house, sees his father washing the BMW; he watches the patterns of water as they splash over the gravel, carving rivulets down the side of the hill. It makes him thirsty. He wants to feel the cool silky stream on his sweating skin. He slips off his running shoes and socks, drops them in the sand by the front door. On a flat rock near the steps is a pile of tiny snail shells. The beginnings of a bracelet. Nikki's work, no doubt.

"How was your run?" His father turns to smile at him.

"Good. Great." He smiles back. Picking up a clean rag from the ground, he steps over to work on the trunk. Any minute now the dinner bell will ring. Each evening his mother comes outside the kitchen door to give the rope three long pulls. *Let the games begin.*

Well, it won't happen again tonight. He's not sure exactly how he'll prevent it, but he won't fall for that same line of questioning that got him into trouble before. *How do you think Van Gogh made his living?* Something on that order, he thinks it was.

He glances up at Davey's window. He's sitting there, looking down at them.

"Wanna help?" he asks.

"No, thanks."

His father laughs, as his brother's head disappears from view.

"Not what you call task-oriented."

"Lazy-Ass-type Renaissance Man," Derek says, polishing the trunk of the Bimmer and staring at his reflection in the shiny surface. *All will be well.* This is his mantra, of late. About going to art school. About Camilla, and all of it. *Chill out. Don't borrow trouble. All will be well.*

DAILY BREAD

SUMMERS UP HERE are not usually that hard to take. But it does seem they are getting steamier as the lake levels recede. Lake Michigan is lower than it's been in the last ten years. The towns of Charlevoix and Petoskey and Traverse City are crowded with people traveling north, trying to escape the heat.

Only they didn't escape it this year. And this afternoon, the meeting of the Elections Board runs long. The chairman finally heaves himself up out of his chair in exasperation: "Listen, I know what Mr. Average Voter's gonna say. He's gonna say why should I pay for some fancy GPS system, when I don't even own a frickin' cell phone?"

It seems to Hugh that he has explained the situation a hundred times: that, if the vote goes down in November and there's no money, they are still legally obligated to install the system. His patience nearly exhausted, he glances at his watch: It's four o'clock. *One more time.*

"It's a federal mandate. We need to try to make the ballot language palatable. If we can do that, we've at least got a chance at having it pass, Jack."

But it's too hot, and the committee is out of the mood, so once again the meeting ends without a decision being made. Another afternoon wasted.

His desktop is clean when he arrives back at his office. Fredda has sorted the folders and stacked them neatly on the windowsill. Only one more call to make and he's caught up with daily business. Maybe he can leave a little early, go home and take a swim at Bailey's beach. He tries the Ann Arbor number again: the worried secretary. The line is still busy.

He dials Karen's cell phone; no answer. She and Becky are probably still in the midst of bathing suit buying. Still, he wishes she'd keep the thing on; he likes to be able to reach her.

He picks up this week's copy of the *Great*

Lakes Pilot. He likes to glance through it and look for real estate. He keeps trying to get his mother-in-law to move up here from Traverse City. If he could find something good and reasonable, he thinks he could win her over.

"I can't see paying more money for a house that won't be as nice as the one I have now," Hannah says. "Anyway, what would I do up there, with all of my friends down here?"

"Make new ones?" She's as social a creature as he's ever met. And why wouldn't she want to live closer to her daughter and her granddaughter? For his part, he'd much rather have her here in Blessed; then he could stop worrying about that drive every time Karen went down to visit.

The telephone rings and he picks it up.

"DeWitt here."

"Hugh, listen. I think I got the wording." It's Jack Drawbaugh, the chairman of the Elections Board. "Keep it simple. *Emergency Dispatch.* Use it right up front. That's what it's about, right? Helping EMS find 'em faster. Who'd vote against that?"

"Sounds good to me, Jack." Wasn't that his original suggestion? What was wrong with it two months ago?

"Okay, we're going with that. I'll call Bennett and the rest. No sense having another meeting."

Amen to that. He hangs up, hearing Ian's voice

out in the hall; not loud but with some urgency to it. Stepping out of his office he sees Fredda at the counter, leaning across it to clutch the hands of a wiry man with a mane of roan-colored hair. Coby LaChappelle. What's he doing in here? Hugh hasn't seen him since last winter, when Coby and his brother Harmon got into a fight during a drinking bout up at the Captain's Corner. The man is sweating and pale; his hair looks wet.

". . . he goes away, never tells me nothin'! I don't hear from him, I figure he's pissed off!"

"Calm down, Coby," Fredda soothes. "Here, sit."

Coby's eyes seek Hugh's, and he starts toward him. "Allus somethin', y'know? It was a goddamn *toolshed,* fer crissake! Who cares where the stain comes from? I mean if it comes from Harold's up at the corner or from someplace in *goddamn Sweden?*"

"What's up, Coby?" He keeps his voice calm, but the old man's anxiety is not to be contained. He presses his hands to his head.

"I swear, I didn't have no idea, Hugh! No fuckin' idea!"

"Start from the beginning, will you?"

"They're *dead,*" Coby says, his voice tipping into anger.

"Who's dead, Coby?" Hugh asks. "Did something happen to Harmon?"

"Harmon's not in this!" His eyes look wildly around the room. "Never tells me to check on the place, never tells me nothin'! So I didn't! Not for weeks I ain't been up there!" His body trembles, as if from an inner chill. Fredda brings a glass of water, and together Hugh and Ian lead him around to a chair.

"I swear, I didn't go no further than inside the doorway! I could see 'em from there! I wasn't goin' any further into that room!" He looks up. "You got to come, Hugh. You got to come right away. There's not the likes of it, not ever in this world."

STEPHEN

He comes down to the beach just in time to see the two men shuffling through the shallows; they pretend not to notice him. The piece of decking they are trundling is balanced across two giant truck-tire inner tubes. They are busy at their task, beer guts flopping over baggy trunks. *Assholes!*

In his T-shirt, swim trunks, and tennis shoes he lounges beside the tall pine tree at the edge of the beach, watching them while adrenaline charges through his veins. He'd predicted it, but he didn't expect it quite this soon. *Who do they think they are, anyway?*

He wishes he wasn't so hungover. The inside of his mouth tastes like dirty pennies, after last night. He's been babying himself all day. Right now he's drinking a can of beer, trying to stabilize his insides. Another few minutes of lying in the hammock and he would've missed this entire scene.

The huge hunk of wood is weighing heavily on the truck tires; they barely break the surface of the water. It's a tough, sweaty job for these two out-of-shape clowns to pull off. They know he's there watching, of course, but they don't let on. The tanned, hairy one calls out to his friend: "Watch you don't trip over the sandbar there."

Stephen ambles down to the shore. The two have to move very slowly. Their burden requires them to stop every now and then in order to let the displaced water catch up with them. The decking nearly slides off the truck tires at one point and back into the water. *How great would that be?* He concentrates on that outcome while drinking his beer.

Last night at the beach fire he told Dennis and the rest about how he and Derek had been working on the dock when these two dudes showed up and spotted the piece of ship's planking—a good fifty feet in length—curving gently out into the lake. It had been there since the dock was built, submerged in the shallow water. But these two had acted as if they'd discovered a hunk of the *Titanic*.

"Hey, we've been lookin' for that," one of them said to Derek. "It used to be down by our place."

"It's part of a shipwreck," the fat one said. "Could be worth a chunk of money someday."

"It's been down here for a while," Derek had said amiably. "I guess they do move around some in the water. During the winter. With the ice and all."

The two had turned their backs on Derek, conferring and stretching their arms below the surface, testing the weight of the sunken derelict. It appeared to be too heavy to lift. As they headed off down the beach, Derek gave them a friendly wave.

"Those dicks think they own that thing," he had told Derek. "They're gonna try and take it back." Derek hadn't believed him.

Now Stephen is standing at the edge of the lake; he's harder to ignore. Fatboy looks over at him. "We're movin' this thing back," he says. "Where it belongs."

"How do you figure?" Stephen asks, imitating Derek's amiable drawl.

"It came from our beach. We been sittin' on it

for ten years. Before it moved itself on down here."

"Guess you don't read the papers, huh? That's a felony. Some guy's on trial down in Cleveland for moving a hunk of driftwood in Lake Erie."

Fatboy smirks. "You'll just hafta call the cops on us, I guess."

"The state don't give a shit about a fuckin' piece of deadwood," the hairy one says scornfully.

"Turns out they do," Stephen says. "Where they wash up is where they're supposed to stay. Museums won't even take the stuff anymore. Might cost you a thousand bucks if anybody found out. I guess you could always play *dumb*. Like you didn't know."

"Aren't you the smart little faggot, though?"

"Son of a *bitch*," the hairy one mutters. Stephen turns his back on them, strips off his T-shirt. He wades out into hip-deep water; it feels cool and silky against his thighs. He dives in, swimming with long, smooth strokes underwater. When he comes up, the men are fifty yards away, slouching along the shoreline, heading north with their booty. *Fucking pirates*. He strokes out into deeper water, flipping to his back and staring upward into the bowl of blue sky. He thinks about his brother. *How can a guy this smart be so dumb about people?* He'll be totally shocked when he tells him that his prediction about these two jerkoffs was right on the money.

Derek's innocence never fails to amaze him. In some ways he guesses it can be a good trait. But most of the time it is his worst fault. Anybody can walk right into Derek's life and take advantage. He has tried to show him how wimpy it is to always look on the good side of people. Starting with Dad. Dad doesn't give a shit whether or not you think well of him; Dad just wants to get his own way. How can Derek put up with Dad's bullshit? Last night at dinner he wanted to step in and say, "Will you *please* tell the guy to take a flying leap?" But it's pointless. Derek doesn't get it. It's in his nature to be trusting. Too trusting.

I can't stay here this whole friggin' summer, he thinks suddenly. He swims back toward shore and stands up, wiping the hair out of his eyes. Denny had planted the seed last night. "Boring town, boring people, boring options," he said. "Nobody lives here but social retards and old people." "Then why do you stay?" he had asked. Denny just grinned. "Because I'm a social retard. And my dad runs my life."

He can't let this happen to him. It's bad enough he'll be spending the next three weeks with all of them. He'll have to figure out some way to escape, even if it's only for a few hours.

Close quarters with the family always takes its toll, because he's the only one who gives a damn about having any autonomy. Once in a while they do manage to unite—usually over something petty and meaningless, like eating at McDonald's instead of some fancy restaurant Dad has in mind—but then he pouts. *Mopes* is a better word for it—he's the champion *moper* when he doesn't get his way. And giving him a fucking inch is like handing over every bit of territory you possess. It was stupid to think he could survive this whole summer trapped up here. It was bad timing, getting the OUIL. Now he can't even drive a car until the end of August. Maybe Derek-Do-Right will give him a ride back to Ann Arbor, and he can find a job somewhere, mowing lawns or teaching tennis at the club.

Dad may as well get used to being pissed off at him. He has already decided he's not going to college after he graduates. He couldn't get into a decent school anyway, with his grades. For sure they're not good enough for Michigan. And he's not interested in having his life programmed anyway; look at where that's gotten Derek. Screwing up is one way out of that. And it's something he's good at.

Fatboy and his friend have disappeared around the curve, and the beach is deserted. He hoists himself onto the dock, sits with his feet in the water, finishing off his beer. He will miss the evenings, miss sailing with Denny. That's about all. One thing he has to admit, though; living with Big Ed Norbois has prepared him for meeting any challenges life has to offer.

TIME STOPPED

I NEED TO GO home," Coby says. He's sitting, hunched over, in the backseat of the patrol car. "I gotta go home, Hugh."

"We'll get you home, Coby," Hugh says.

"This the turnoff?" Ian asks. "Coby, is this the place?"

"Yeah, between them two pillars." He is much subdued now, hands clasped in his lap, hair flattened against his forehead. A shiver hikes over his thin shoulders.

"Shouldn't of gone up there," he mutters to himself.

"You notice any tracks in the driveway when you first drove in?" Ian asks.

"Not that I saw."

"What kind of work were you doing for this guy?" Hugh asks.

"Just odd jobs. Been workin' for him ever since they first started buildin' the place. Don't hear nothin' from him, so I figure he's got somebody else. Fine. But he never asks for his key back . . ."

"How long since you last talked to him?"

"Mebbe a month . . ." Coby draws a shuddery breath. "Never seen anythin' like it, Hugh . . . You don't go in there without some kinda protection. It's god-awful . . ."

The switchback lane that leads to the top of the bluff opens onto a neat gravel surround bordered with stones. Behind it is a fenced garden. The soil is cracked and dry. The tomato plants are the only ones flourishing. Everything else looks limp, wilted from the heat.

On the gravel drive is a black BMW, parked next to a blue Chevrolet Suburban and a gray Passat. Both cars are dusty, covered with tiny green pellets—the dropped seedpods from tall Norway pines. The house, set slightly back from the drive, is made of giant honey-colored logs, with a massive front door of oak slabs varnished to a glossy dark mirror.

Hugh opens the car door and the stench hits him full in the face—appalling even from thirty feet away. He hits the trunk button as he climbs out, and he and Ian rummage through the trunk in search of surgical masks. They find them and quickly smear two fingers of Vicks VapoRub over the nosepieces.

"I ain't goin' in there," Coby says from the backseat.

"You don't need to," says Hugh. "Just stay put. We'll be back."

Up close, the odor is overwhelming, unmistakable. Hugh slips on protective gloves, hands a pair to Ian. They approach the front door and Hugh twists the knob; it's locked. The drapes on the front windows are tightly closed.

They circle around to the back, passing floor-to-ceiling windows, similarly covered. At the back door they stop. Hugh looks through the window and sees a set of stairs leading up into the kitchen. Coby's keys are still in the lock. Hugh pushes, and the door opens easily. A wave of poisonous air greets them. Ian gives a short, savage grunt.

A small entryway, lined with shelves of sweatshirts, scarves, rain gear, beach towels. Several pairs of sunglasses are piled inside a small cubicle. A wicker basket stacked with silverware sits on the kitchen table; next to it, napkins and a set of salt and pepper shakers. The kitchen lights are on; the rest of the house is in semidarkness.

Hugh climbs the steps into the kitchen. Through the doorway into the hall he makes out two mounded shapes. He walks through the kitchen into the hallway; more bodies come into view. One of them, the head hanging, sits in a wingback chair. Another is lying on the tiled entranceway at the front door.

Curled around a table leg is the body of a young teenaged boy. He is guessing this from the clothing, but it's hard to be sure. The head is under the table and Hugh can see what looks like a bullet hole through the center of the forehead.

Hugh makes his way across the room to the body in front of the door. It's a woman lying face-down in a pool of black blood. Her shorts and underpants are pulled below her knees, and the swollen flesh of her body has split in a hundred places; a viscous liquid seeping through the cracks. A parade of maggots moves busily over the surfaces.

The body in the wing chair is that of a man, dressed in khakis and a T-shirt, loafers without socks. His hands are at his sides. The white T-shirt has two black exploding flowers in the center. His feet rest beneath the sturdy wooden card table in front of him. Across the table a deck of playing cards is scattered; some of the cards are on the floor.

"Jesus, Hugh," Ian says. "The stairway. Look over here."

More black bloodstains smeared on the wall. They follow them up the stairs into a front bedroom. Two more bodies are sprawled before an open closet. On the floor inside is a 30.06 rifle and, next to it, a box of spilled shells. *Maybe that's what these two were heading for.* They look to be young men. Dressed in shorts and T-shirts like the man downstairs in the chair. Bullet holes, like angry eyes, in the backs of their heads.

Hugh steps to the window, yanking open the curtains. Below on the ground he can see Coby, standing next to the patrol car, stooped over, hands pressed against his face.

"This is fucking awful," Ian murmurs behind the mask. "I think I'm gonna throw up."

"Go outside," Hugh says grimly. He heads for the stairs, reaching into his pocket for the cell phone. *Call Doc DeVere, that's the first order of business. Then Harry Rose.* He needs to get some evidence techs up here. He needs to get the place cordoned off before Coby tells anybody about it. He doesn't want people showing up here who haven't been invited. Nobody else is going to have to look at this, not if he can help it.

DAVID

THAT'S IT. The death card. Three times in a row. How can he not tell people about this? It's too damn weird. And tomorrow, when they take off in the plane to Canada, and he looks down, all he'll be seeing is miles of green water teeming with slivers of white foam. Waves always look like they're alive to him, and not very friendly. Not his choice to fly. Even if he hadn't just gotten this notice.

An itch on the knuckle of his forefinger. Right on cue. He rubs the knuckle with the thumb of his left hand, hard enough to roughen the skin. One, two, three, four little white lines. Four days, and none of them will be around anymore. Okay, that gives him some time to prepare for it. He knows it's pointless to tell Dad; he'd just freak like he always does, and threaten to send him out to Pine Rest. Sometimes his mother will at least listen to him, even if she doesn't believe in predictions of the future. And she will occasionally change her plans, when it doesn't prove to be too inconvenient. She'll change her route to the store, for instance, or wait until the afternoon to run errands. But she won't help him with this one; it's too damn big.

So be it. When it's your turn, you go. The laws of the cosmos apply here. Maybe you can stretch things out sometimes, or slip through the cracks, but sooner or later, your time's up. It's definitely a timing thing, like musical chairs. All around you people are falling, while for some odd reason, you keep getting to sit down. Until one day you don't get to anymore.

What things could he arrange in the next few days, without arousing suspicion? He could maybe get sick tonight and they'd have to delay the trip. No. Dad would just say he'd be sick whether he's lying in bed here or in Banff, so what's the difference? Besides, the number four is what's significant. They might not even be flying on Day Four, they might be walking across a street or taking a boat trip on Lake Louise. It could be something like that he has to watch out for—a bus, or a grand piano hurtling down out of a window.

He glances toward his own window, sees Derek coming down the path. He's got his running gear on. *Tell Derek about it.* No. Derek tends to pay a little too much attention. He's always weighing the possibility that his baby brother is a nutcase. Truth is, nobody in this family takes him seriously about this stuff. But then, why should they? The news is never good—like they're going to win the lottery, or one of them is on the verge of discovering the key to curing cancer.

And yet, didn't he predict the day Grandma Pearl would die? On the fifteenth day of January in the year 2002. He had it written down in his notebook. He's been writing these things down ever since he was ten years old; the same age that Nikki is now. He wonders if she ever has anything like this going on in her head. He doubts it. She's too much of a flea brain.

He wishes sometimes that he could just ignore this stuff. But how do you ignore the death card when it comes up three times in a row? Sitting cross-legged on the bed, he shuffles the cards. The late afternoon sun warms the bedspread under his knees. Not much point in doing it again. Even if it comes up differently, he won't believe it. He stacks the cards, carefully wrapping them in the silk scarf he took from his mother's drawer. Funny she never missed it. But then, she has so many, wears them tied around her neck or in her hair. And it was near the bottom of the pile, so maybe it wasn't one she really cared about.

He lifts the corner of the mattress and tucks the wrapped deck as far under as he can reach. Not that people are snoopy in this house, they're not; they could actually care less. You could leave something sitting right out in plain sight and nobody'd see it. They are the least curious group of people that he knows. Not that he doesn't love them, he does; his brothers have always looked after him, even if they talk down to him and treat him like a baby. And Nikki is the one that he looks after and talks down to. In the main, this is a nice group of people, who treat him well. As an extraterrestrial being, he has certainly landed in a most pleasant situation.

Although it sometimes bothers him that things are somewhat *off* between his dad and his brothers. But that isn't his problem. *Best to be independent of everyone in this crazy world of humanoids.*

He needs to have his options ready, however, when the time comes to make his move. He reaches over, picks up today's newspaper from the floor. The article about extrasolar planets orbiting nearby stars is interesting; he needs to read it again. Gazing at the photo in the middle of the page he wonders if he's right about which planet it is that he came from. He's pretty sure it's the one orbiting a star called HD160691. Fifty light-years or some three hundred trillion miles away. Only they're wrong when they say it's a gas giant, that it can't possibly support life. The history of his people has extended farther back in time than the planet Earth, and scientists here haven't yet developed the techniques and machinery to equal those of his own planet's interferometers. Well, time will tell.

"Hey! Want to help make a compost pile in the woods?"

Derek has arrived at the back door and is looking up at him.

"What for?" he asks, annoyed that his voice comes out like a whiny kid's. "We can't finish it before dinner."

"A little exercise won't kill you."

Even though he is some three million universe years older than they are, he can't seem to get his brothers to treat him with the proper respect.

"I got to find my shoes . . ."

"Your shoes are down here on the steps. We're not building the great pyramid. Get your butt down here. Don't make me come up and get you, Dimwit."

"Why don't you ask Nikki?"

"Because she's a little gurrll, and you're a big, tough *lumberstud*."

He slides the newspaper under the mattress, next to the deck of cards. Maybe he's about to head back to HD160691. If that's so, he won't be able to avert the disaster that awaits them. And it's right then, that he can't. It's always good to keep up with NASA findings; sometimes they give you a hint about the future. *You can't afford to get behind on this stuff.* He'll go over the article again later tonight, after he's packed for the trip, when he has some spare time.

THE CLOCK IS
TICKING

CRIME LAB, this is Gellar."

"Hi, Mack," Hugh says. "Thanks for taking my call. I've got a multiple homicide here."

"You're kidding me. In *Blessed?* The natives finally got restless?"

The Grayling State Police Post, off I-75 mid-state, is the busiest cop shop around, where everyone goes for help. Communities like Hugh's don't rate high on Mack's list. He likes to make fun of the misconduct that passes for criminal behavior there. "The knave of hearts, he stole some tarts," is how he characterizes it. But he's been an invaluable friend ever since he and Hugh attended Police Academy together.

"Summer people," Hugh says. "Looks like a whole family. And it's not fresh."

"How not fresh?"

"Three weeks, possibly longer."

"Jesus, that sounds nasty. What was it—a robbery?"

"More like someone just came through and mowed 'em down. I'm going to need techs. Plus gas masks, equipment, whatever you've got available."

"Well, you know my situation. They're all in Ann Arbor. That body they found last week took just about everything I had."

The serial coed killings. They've been going on for more than a year at the University of Michigan and surrounding areas. Now the fourth victim, found in a dumpster in Washtenaw County, has caused a furor, with everyone from parents to professors to state congressmen screaming for vengeance.

"I get it," Hugh says. "But I've only got Harry and the Doc here, and they've never dealt with anything like this."

"All right, I'll do my best," Mack says. "I could maybe round up a couple of guys. Doesn't sound like there's any big rush, though. How's tomorrow morning at nine?"

"Fine. Just give me whatever you have, I'd appreciate it. I'll get things lined up so we're ready for you."

He hangs up and dials into the office. "Fredda, make up a duty roster: I need two men every four hours around the clock. Tell Ollie LeFave to bring his dogs. Then get Doc DeVere and Harry Rose. Tell them I need them right away."

"Is it bad?"

"Worse than bad," he says. "Call Karen and leave her a message, will you? Tell her I'll be late tonight."

"How's Coby holding up?"

He glances over his shoulder. "Coby split. I don't blame him. Tell Harry we need to get things set up tonight. Grayling's sending a couple of techs over in the morning."

He turns toward the house and something catches his eye—a buff-colored square of cardboard in the window, fastened over a pane with duct tape. It's half-hidden behind a boxwood shrub next to the front door. He pulls his mask back in place, moving forward and bending down to get a closer look. A neat job, very carefully done. He looks around the area: no footprints. In fact it looks as though the ground has been swept clean. A slurry of dirt and sticks curves through the flat stones at the edge of the walkway. Someone recently did some watering.

Bushy transplants of juniper and blue spruce are spread across the front of the house. And Christmas fern—one of Karen's favorites. Odd—this scrap of cardboard in the corner of the window. Why would a guy spending thousands of dollars on landscaping leave a job like that undone?

Bending down, he scrapes gently with a penknife at the edge of the tape. It takes him several minutes to loosen the four corners; beneath the cardboard are two round holes just inches apart.

He steps carefully out of the bushes. Moving around to the back, he re-enters the house through the kitchen door.

Inside, the stillness is heavier than a mere absence of activity; it carries the weight of death. Each time in the presence of it, he has felt this peculiar heaviness entering his own body. *They will have to burn the place down. The smell is in the walls; it's permanent.*

Making his way slowly through the living room, keeping his eyes straight ahead, he approaches the draped front windows and parts the curtains until the damaged pane is visible. Bending down to examine it, he then turns toward the body slumped in the chair. The trajectory looks right. He takes a pencil from his pocket, inserts it into the lower hole. It angles slightly upward, aimed directly at the black flower blooming on the man's chest.

One victim shot from outside; the first one, obviously. Hard to imagine a lone gunman capable of doing this kind of damage. Was it some kind of a gang killing?

And then he really looks at the mounds lying at the man's feet. Next to the boy's body is another. A face dark with decay; the stomach grossly distended. Hugh's eyes focus on the black-and-white-checked sunsuit, the thin, outflung arm. Blond pigtails tied with white ribbons. *Oh hell.*

HOUSE AND HOME

IT'S AFTER MIDNIGHT when he pulls into the driveway. A light rain is falling, and Karen is there, waiting. She puts her arms around him without a word.

"Becky asleep?"

"Yes, of course. Are you okay?"

"I'm fine. Fredda called you?"

"She left a message. I called her when we got home. Hugh, she said there were kids . . ."

"Yeah, four of them. Honey, I have to take a shower."

She follows him up to the bedroom.

"It's all over town," she says.

"Yeah, I figured. People started showing up after dinner. Coby must've stopped at every house on his way back."

He steps into the bathroom, takes off his clothes, turns on the shower. He needs to get his head under the water, wash away the weight from his chest and back.

"What have you been doing all this time?" she asks.

"We spent a few hours going through the woods with the dogs. LeFave and me."

"Cadaver dogs?"

"Yeah. Luke and Rust. God, LeFave loves those two like they're his kids." He comes out of the shower, and she hands him a towel. "Then it starts to rain. Geez, after all these weeks. Perfect timing." He glances down at the thick, pale blue of the cloth around his torso. "These new?" he asks.

"About time, don't you think?"

"Blue. That mean we're redoing the bath-room?"

"Starting tomorrow. I bought wallpaper, too."

He sits down next to her on the bed, holds her tightly against him, rocking them both back and forth.

"You're sure you're all right." She smooths the wet hair from his forehead.

"Yeah, I'm just tired of telling people to go home, go about their business."

"You can't blame them, Hugh. This is a huge thing."

"I know. You'd think the smell alone'd keep them away. They really don't want to get close to this. Nobody wants to get close to this." He gets up, roughly drying himself, grabbing a clean T-shirt from his dresser drawer.

"Does that mean you don't want to talk about it?"

"Yeah, I guess so. Not tonight. I gotta be back there early in the morning . . ." He trails off. "I'm sick," he says. "If I tell you, then you'll be sick. What good will that do? I'd rather talk about the fucking wallpaper."

She comes to him, puts her arms around him, kisses his shirt over his breastbone. For a moment his chin rests against her hair; it smells freshly washed, with the faint odor of flowers. *Freesia.* He loves the sound of that word, her favorite perfume.

"You hungry?" she asks. "I made some gingerbread."

"Okay, yeah."

Together they walk arm in arm down to the kitchen, where the light from the small table lamp illuminates the cover of the book she's reading. He picks it up.

"Haven't you read this already?"

"I'm reading it again."

"I can never figure that out. You know how it ends. What's the point?"

She shrugs. "Sometimes they end differently when you read them a second time."

He grins. "You talking down to me again?"

She slides a piece of cake onto a plate, hands it across the table with a fork. "Sorry, no applesauce."

"That's okay." Suddenly he is ravenous. He wolfs the dense sweetness down with large bites. "I love this stuff," he says. "I love *you*."

She laughs. Her hair, tucked neatly behind her ears, is exactly the same shade as his daughter's— a dark halo in the backlight from the lamp. He wipes his hands carefully on the napkin she hands him.

"You think you've seen everything," he says. "I guess that never happens, huh?" And then, unbelievably, he yawns; despite everything, despite the grim scene he cannot shake from inside his head. "Geez, I gotta get some sleep."

They go upstairs, Karen leading the way. Hugh leaves the kitchen light on, can't bear the thought of the house in darkness, not tonight. He stops outside the open doorway to Becky's room.

His daughter lies, asleep, on her side, her slight body curved into the profile of a quarter moon. A mouth breather. He can hear the air as it whistles softly through her teeth. He enters and sits on the edge of her bed, pulling the sheet over her bare shoulders.

Pale, translucent skin, milky-looking in the light from the hallway. Karen is strict with the sunscreen, won't let her even walk down the road without it. Skin cancer, now the bogeyman of every mother's nightmare. *Life is fraught with danger on all sides. And all that went before can so easily become irrelevant.*

That is the horror of it. Tonight, walking the woods with LeFave and his dogs—parallel, six feet apart, searching for anything that might be of use—he couldn't stop thinking about the people inside. Voiceless, silent; their lives and daily tasks, their ambitions and hopes, their fears and their histories—all irrelevant now. Worse than that. This act, this moment of their lives, has now become the single most important thing about them. Everything they've done, or might have done in the future, pales before their collective deaths. *Brutal. Grisly. Sinister. Slaughter.* He can see the headlines tomorrow, in every paper in the state.

Rising quickly from his daughter's bed, he leans down to kiss her—gently, so as not to disturb her sleep. Her hand reaches up to touch his face, but she isn't awake; her eyes don't open.

The air coming through the window is soft, fragrant with the odor of Colorado spruce. He planted the tree out there, beneath her window, on the day of her birth. And another one for Petey, next to it. Both of them straight and strong, bursting with new growth each spring. *Expect the worst. Then you won't be surprised. Don't let the goblins get you.* Why these morbid, cynical slogans about life rising always to the surface? He looks at his watch: 1:30 A.M. Turning abruptly, he moves away, willing himself toward mindless, dreamless sleep.

LOCAL GOSSIP

HUGH IS OUT of bed at five-thirty, catching the alarm before it goes off. He dons a clean uniform, making a mental note to tell Karen to send yesterday's to the cleaners. No, she'll do it without his prompting. He looks over and she is lying on her stomach, eyes open, watching him.

"Could be a long day," he says. "I might be late again. I'll call you." He bends to kiss her, and she reaches up to pull him close.

"Don't work too hard." This said in her stern, wifely voice.

"Are you worried? Hey, don't worry about me."

At the kitchen table, he pours a cup of coffee and forces himself to sit for a moment, organizing his thoughts. Then he reaches for the telephone. Kevin answers on the first ring.

"Watkins here, yeah."

"It's me, Kev. You find out anything yet?"

"Yep. Edward Norbois owns a company called Challenge Press here in town. He's a big honcho in the ad business. That's the whole family— mother and father and four kids." Kevin sighs. "Like we don't have enough going on down here right now. What else d'you need from me?"

"Somebody has to go over and tell the secretary. She called me yesterday. Her name's Anne Ransome." He fishes the piece of paper from his wallet, reads off the telephone number.

"Okay, I'll take care of it. You sending the bodies down to Blodgett?"

"Yeah. Gonna be a few days, though, I think."

"Now you can have reporters around your neck for a change," Kevin says. "Fucking albatrosses is what they are. Get this latest thing: After we send the fourth body over to the chapel, we get a call from the funeral director. Somebody walks in off the street and asks to take a picture of the body. For the family, he says. He talks the handyman into letting him into the viewing room and then gets pissed because it's a closed casket.

'Couldn't you fix her up so she'd be okay for viewing?' By the time the funeral director finds out about it, the guy's long gone. Turns out the family never requested any such thing."

"Spooky," Hugh says.

"It's bad, Hugh. I've got parents calling me all day long."

He doesn't blame Kevin for being preoccupied; a coed killer on the loose, with no leads and no arrests in sight. The news has hit national TV. In another month or so the fall semester at Michigan begins, bringing with it memories of that first murder. Kevin Watkins, as chief of the Ann Arbor Police Department, is on overload. He doesn't have time for Hugh's problems.

Hugh hangs up and dials the number of Blodgett Hospital in Grand Rapids, asks for Dr. Shaw. Only a little after six, but he knows Billy will be at his desk; seems as if he always is, no matter what the hour.

"Forensics."

Billy listens as Hugh explains the situation.

"Wow. Bodies in massive degeneration, that'll be interesting. Okay, we're ready whenever you are."

"Depends on how many evidence techs I get from Grayling," Hugh says. "I'll call you when the bodies are in transit."

One of the things about this job is learning to appreciate life's ambiguities. The idea that to some people bodies in massive degeneration would fascinate rather than repulse is one of them.

His last call is to the Carlisle Funeral Chapel.

"Terry, this is Hugh."

"Yeah, I was expecting to hear from you last night. I got a call from Harmon LaChappelle. He said it happened up on the bluff. Said Sarah Clement found the bodies . . . ?"

"No," says Hugh, "Coby found 'em." News always travels fast up here and with a predictable measure of unreliability. "Listen, we're going to need transportation to Blodgett Hospital. Six body bags with metal caskets."

"Six to G.R., got it," Terry says. "So Coby found them? That's interesting. I thought he got fired from that job."

"Where'd you hear that?"

"Can't remember. Probably from his brother. They're the eyes and ears of the world up here. So it's bad, huh?"

"Yeah. The bodies have been up there for a while. You don't want to use your hearse."

"When do you want me?"

"Could be as late as Wednesday. I'll talk to you as soon as I know more. Maybe later today."

He refills his coffee cup at the counter. *Why would Harmon LaChappelle tell Terry it was*

Sarah Clement who found the bodies? He will never understand these oddball brothers, if he lives to be a hundred.

Karen comes into the kitchen and Hugh smiles up at her.

"Tell Becky I'm sorry I didn't get to see her new clothes last night."

"We have time," she says. "Just remember. There's respite care available here, should you need it. You just have to ask."

"I will, I promise."

At the bottom of the bluff, between the two brick pillars, he sees Stu Hamilton's black panel truck waiting for him. The gold seal is painted on the door: *Emmet County Review—A Newspaper of Quality.* Stu's weekly is the principal reporting vehicle for Blessed and the surrounding areas.

"You didn't call me last night," Stu says, as Hugh gets out of the patrol car. "I had to find it out from Jules Charbonneau."

"I didn't get home until after midnight."

"How much time have we got before the pundits arrive?"

"Not much, I'm betting," says Hugh. "Maybe this afternoon. How did Jules hear about it? No, don't tell me."

"Everybody knows about it," Stu says. "Okay if I follow you up there?"

"Yeah. But you won't like it."

"No, I don't suppose." He indicates the white surgical mask hanging from the rearview mirror of his truck. "I'm prepared, though. Heard the guy didn't show up at work after his vacation was over. Their plane's been sitting at the Pellston airport since the twentieth of June. Did you know he was a pilot? Flew his own Cessna. Those things are expensive as hell. The family must've been loaded."

"Jesus, where'd you get all that?" Hugh smiles thinly. Stu is a solid reporter and his contempt for downstate papers is well known. He won't be scooped on this one. *Get some deputies down there to handle traffic,* Hugh thinks. Only seven-fifteen in the morning and already it's Grand Central Station. Soon it will be a full-time job just keeping the gawkers away. An entire family wiped out. Plus, all that money. A big story; bigger than this town has ever handled on its own.

LECTURE TIME

THE PARKING AREA is stacked with squad cars and miscellaneous vehicles. *Keeping traffic moving up here will be a problem as well.*

Harry Rose, his one and only evidence technician, meets him at the back door of the log house, while Stu gives Hugh the high sign, staying discreetly back; he'll find his way inside on his own.

The Grayling contingency has arrived early. Some of the drapes have been pulled back, and Hugh sees the men walking around inside, looking like exotic insects in their blue uniforms and beetle-like masks.

Harry puffs on a cigarette, the mask dangling loosely from his other hand. "D'you believe the fucking furnace was on the whole time? Where's Boland and his camera? We're gonna need him pretty quick."

As if on cue a car door slams and, moments later, Ned Boland lopes across the yard carrying his black canvas bag over one shoulder. Dragging a mask from the bag, he pulls it over his face. "Hey, fellas, it seriously stinks out here."

Harry tosses his cigarette, steps on it, retrieves the butt, and slips it into his shirt pocket. "Okay, the quicker we're done, the quicker we get to go somewhere else."

Together the three enter the house. Two men are taking blood samples at separate ends of the living room, their heads bowed over trays of rubber-stoppered tubes. Notebooks, pens, and measuring tapes lie scattered about. Sunlight pours through the windows with a fiery intensity, coating the corpses with liquid bronze. The yellow chalk outlining the bodies looks like the boundaries of some weird kids' game.

Hugh hears footsteps overhead. "Did we get some extras?" he asks. The taller of the two evidence techs steps toward him, extending his hand.

"Tom Maher. Good to meet you. Yeah, a couple of our guys got back early. So, what do you think? Looks like an execution-style operation so far. Everybody with bullet holes in the backs of their heads. All but the little girl. Somebody decided to beat hers in with a hammer."

Hugh's stomach turns over; he takes the evidence sheet that Maher hands him, glances quickly over it, keeping his eyes carefully averted from the small, black-and-white bundle on the floor.

"I think," Maher says, "along with your man, we can wrap this whole thing up in two days."

"Good," says Hugh. "When will you want the truck here to take the bodies?"

Maher shrugs. "I'd say barring any complications, around five o'clock tomorrow afternoon."

Ian beckons to him from the kitchen. "We got a slight problem, Hugh. Coby's down at the Captain's Corner, filling people's ears with some tall tales."

"Okay, ice him," Hugh says. "And get a traffic detail on 119."

"Anything else?"

"We need to start canvassing the ridge. I'll go north and you head south. After you take care of Coby."

Hugh heads down to Sarah Clement's place.

"You're not here to move me into town, are you?" She's sitting on her front porch, as if she's been waiting for him.

"You mean because of what happened? No. Who told you that?"

"Coby was here, rattling on about some homicidal maniac hiding out on the bluff. I told him we don't have maniacs or drifters in Emmet County. The climate's too tough for 'em. If you ask me, that man hasn't got the sense of a gopher. He lives in some dream world. His own wife will tell you that."

"You can't put someone in jail for being a windbag, Sarah," Hugh says, although this is precisely what he has just done.

"He hasn't been right in the head since his son died," Sarah says, her voice softening slightly. "Going on eight years now. That kid was maybe fifteen at the time, too young to be riding a motorcycle. Coby gave him everything, that was the problem. And those daughters of his, smart as whips they were, never got but the time of day out of him." She shakes her head.

"You and Coby's wife still friends?"

"Used to be. Then they both got too loony for me to tolerate. Not all at once, but you know, over time . . ." She taps the side of her forehead, but she doesn't seem happy about having told him this. Sitting there, staring woefully into the past.

Hugh sits down beside her. "Got a few questions for you."

Her head snaps up and she gives him a wry grin. "Uh huh. Now come the questions, Mr. Don't Notice Anything."

"You're right, I screwed up, Sarah. How well did you know the Norbois family?"

"Oh, hardly at all. They've been here about four years I guess, maybe five. They bought part of Hark Rayburn's land. Never could see why he sold it off like that. Coulda been a gorgeous wildlife refuge. Instead we got a subdivision. All rich folks from downstate. *New Voh Reesh,* my kids say. Hark told me he was going to deed it back to the state, but I guess he had a better idea."

"Did you know the kids?" he prods gently.

"Not the older ones. And I never did meet him. But she came over to introduce herself and I gave her a few cuttings for her garden. Zebra grass and ribbon grass. She was wanting to put in all native plants. I liked that. Of course her husband might've left a little something when he dug up the ground and built that monstrosity . . ." She sighs. "But she was a very nice lady. Came over with her daughter just to say hello. I remember my coneflowers weren't up yet, and I told her to stop back in the fall, I'd dig some for her."

"When was the last time you saw her?"

She thinks a minute. "I'd say sometime in

June. They were on their way into town. That's when I gave her the cuttings."

"Heard anything unusual at all from over that way?"

"You mean like gunshots? I think I'd have noticed that. Then again, my hearing's not what it used to be. Kids think I should get a hearing aid, but I'm not sure there's much worth listening to these days."

"Your hearing seems pretty sharp to me. What do you know about your other neighbors? The ones to the north? Ryback—is that their name?"

"I know they haven't been up yet this summer. They live in Cleveland, Ohio. Wouldn't surprise me if they were to sell the place. Hardly ever use it." Her tone is disapproving. "People buy up here, the first year they're up every weekend, trimming trees and putting in a lawn, so's to make it look like their home in the city. All of a sudden you don't see 'em for months and they hire somebody to mow; then it's been a year since there's a car in the drive. Then they sell. Such a waste." Her tongue clicks sharply against her teeth.

"So what are your plans for your property, Sarah?" he asks her, standing up.

She grins. "Wouldn't you like to know, Mr.

Sheriff DeWitt? You never can tell. I may just decide to live forever."

Some three hundred yards beyond the empty Ryback place is a cream-colored sign with BEGLEY painted on it in tailored black letters. The blue Land Rover, parked close to the house, has its back door open. A kayak is strapped to the roof rack. Hugh pulls up behind the car and gets out, just as a young woman in yellow slacks and a white shirt comes through the open door. She's carrying a cardboard box full of foodstuffs in her arms. She stops dead at the sight of him.

"Lou!"

In an instant, a man with sparse gray hair appears in the doorway behind her. "Help you?" he asks Hugh briskly.

Hugh quickly explains his errand. "We're checking with people in the area. To see if they noticed anything unusual in the past month."

"Sorry. Can't be of much help to you. We just got in. Late last night. Came up from Detroit for the weekend. But we're not staying." He inclines his head backward. "She's pretty upset over this whole thing. Understandable. Terrible tragedy. I didn't know them, but, all the same . . ." While he's talking the woman slips past him to return inside the house. "I was up over the Fourth of July," he says. "That was the first time this year. We never come in June. Weather's too iffy."

Hugh smiles pleasantly. "Long drive up here for nothing last night."

The man's posture tells Hugh he'd like him to vacate the premises. Or maybe Lou Begley is simply used to directing things. It's clear that these two were interrupted; another few minutes and they would have been gone.

"If I could speak with your wife a minute . . ." Hugh says.

"She's not my wife," the man says. "She's a friend of mine. She doesn't know anything about this." The thin mouth snaps closed. No wonder the guy's in such a hurry.

"Then if I could have an address and phone number where you can be reached," Hugh says, "I'll be on my way." He hands Begley his notebook and pen.

Begley takes the stuff, his irritation apparent. He scribbles some lines on the paper, hands it back. "This is all on file at the county clerk's office, by the way. That's my work number. It's the best place to reach me."

Yeah, I'll bet. Hugh thanks the man, climbs into the patrol car. No doubt Mrs. Begley would be interested to know about Lou Begley's friend.

Or maybe not. In any case, with a pile of reporters nosing around, it wouldn't be the ideal place for a quiet tryst.

Tryst. That's quaint. He smiles to himself as he backs down the drive. He's been reading too many of Karen's English mysteries.

A CLOSED BOOK

THEY MEET FOR lunch at the Coney Island. The café, owned by the Charbonneau family, sits at the back of a huge parking lot that is idle now, since Glen's Supermarket closed its doors. Weeds are sprouting in the cracks of the pavement; somebody needs to get out here with a spray can of Roundup, Hugh thinks as he gets out of the patrol car.

Julie Charbonneau is working the counter, as she does every day from six until two. She waves to Hugh from the coffee urn. A big smile for Ian. They sit at the counter, menus in hand.

"People on the south end are packing up," Ian says. "Nobody wants to be anywhere around this thing. I talked to three families who were leaving this morning. Nobody saw any strangers, nobody heard anything unusual, nobody noticed a strange smell. Basically, nobody knows anything. Pretty depressing."

"Yeah, I got the same routine. Plus, nobody seems to have known *them*," Hugh says. "And yet everybody knows about Coby's troubles with them. I've heard that from three different people today."

"I found one thing out," Ian says. "Coby and Harmon LaChappelle both worked on the Norbois cabin while it was being built. Then Harmon got fired for drinking on the job. And Coby was pissed over it. He kept telling people how it didn't pay to get on the bad side of a town, especially with all the things that could go wrong in a house—the septic system, the furnace, hot water heater, et cetera . . ."

"Coby shooting off his mouth again," Hugh says. "He was nearly catatonic yesterday. Why didn't he stay that way?"

"What's going on, Hugh?" Julie asks as she comes toward them. "I don't believe this has happened. Up here? Where people don't even bother to lock their doors at night?"

"That's not smart," Ian says. "You should

bother. That's asking for it, leaving your doors unlocked."

"Well, whoever did it isn't still around, is he?"

"Nobody knows that for sure."

"What's good today, Julie?" Hugh asks.

"Chicago Coney," she says, "and a chocolate malt."

"I'll have it."

"The same," says Ian.

"Jesus, who are you—Joe Friday?" Hugh asks as Julie walks away. "Why don't you just ask her out and be done with it? You know you want to."

"Just because you're my boss," Ian says, "doesn't mean you're not annoying as hell."

Hugh grins. "Just trying to move things along."

"Hugh, you don't think there's a chance either Coby or Harmon had anything to do with this, do you?"

"God, no. Not those two. I'd bet my life on it."

The cell phone at Hugh's belt rings loudly; heads turn along the counter as he pulls it out. "DeWitt here."

"Hugh, it's Kevin. I'm calling from Norbois's office. His secretary wants to talk to you about this. Maybe you ought to think about coming down today."

He glances at his watch. "It's noon now. I can be there by five-thirty."

"Yeah, that'd be good. She'd like to meet with you at her house. Why don't you stop by my place and I'll go over with you?"

He hangs up and Julie returns with their lunches.

Ian eyes his malt gloomily. "I need this like a hole in my head. Why'd I order it? I'm too fat."

"Let's get a second opinion on that," Hugh says. He raises a hand to call Julie back and Hugh slaps it down.

"You honestly believe her old man wants the town deputy making a move on his daughter?"

"I think you're a better man than her ex was. And that's with an eye missing and both legs gone."

Ian laughs. "Gee, that's a pretty picture. Give me a raise, why don't you? I'll think about it."

"Make sure they take prints from the two cars at the cabin," Hugh says. "Then go over and talk to the ground crew at Pellston Airport. Find out if the family had plans for using the Cessna."

"What about the reporters?"

Hugh shrugs. "Tell 'em what we've got."

"Which is basically nothing."

"Be polite. Just don't give them anything they can quote."

"Want me to go talk to Harmon? See if I can find out something?"

"Sure."

"What about Coby? Should I let him out of jail?"

"Not just yet."

Hugh stops at home to pick up a few items to take along for overnight. Karen isn't there. He leaves her a note:

> Had to go to Ann Arbor. Will call
> you from there.

He's on the road by twelve-forty-five, cruising south on 31 with the traffic until he reaches Conway. It takes him less than an hour to reach I-75. Maybe he'll get a different picture of this family when he talks to their neighbors and friends downstate. It's not unusual for people to look for privacy in the place where they vacation; it doesn't mean their life in Ann Arbor would have been equally isolated. But then most people who live on the bluff at least exchange keys, in case of an emergency. So far, it looks like the only person who had a key to the Norbois cabin was Coby LaChappelle. *Damn those two daffy old men. They'll get themselves implicated, one way or another, if only to screw up the investigation. They're the town screwups; they're just fulfilling their destiny.*

Hugh checks the speedometer: steady at sixty-seven. The drive down gives him a good chance to think. Something nags at him about the Norbois family; the fact that they lived for four years on the bluff and yet they don't seem to have been known by anyone. Was it intentional? Did Edward Norbois have some reason for keeping to himself? *Somebody must know these people. Somebody must care that they are dead.*

"This'll work out good," Kevin says, opening the car door and settling in beside Hugh. "I got an hour before I'm due at the meeting."

"What meeting?"

"Another four-county press briefing about the serial killings. We have 'em every week now. There's not one new piece of information that we didn't already give out last week." He shrugs. "They want every damned detail. Then they wonder why the guy is always three jumps ahead of us."

"Whose idea is it? These meetings?"

"Mine."

Hugh laughs. He hasn't seen his friend in six months. *Bulkier than ever.* Immediately he feels a twinge of guilt for noticing. Being top dog in the Ann Arbor Police Department doesn't make for a healthy lifestyle. Too much fast food. Too much banquet chicken. And here he is adding his own burden to Kevin's mix. Aloud he says: "Appreciate your help on this, buddy."

"Don't thank me yet. Here's what I got for you: hardly any family left on either side. Husband and wife were only children; all four sets of grand-parents are dead. Edward Norbois has a couple of cousins who live in Utah, another in Montana."

"So that explains why no relatives reported them missing."

"Nobody was concerned except the secretary. This lady is dying to talk to you. Apparently she suspected foul play but didn't know what to do about it. Says Norbois never went anywhere with-out keeping in close touch with her. She's been worried about them. Here, take Washtenaw and go south." He gives a long sigh. "What a lousy fucking day. The Levin girl's funeral is tomorrow. I'm posting three detectives there."

"You think your guy might show up?"

"Who knows? It's worth a try. I'm sure it was him wanting to see her body at the funeral chapel. I swear, Hughie, if I have to go to one more fam-ily with this kinda news it's gonna kill me."

"You've got no doubts about this girl's murder being connected with the others," Hugh says.

"None whatever. Raped, strangled, stabbed in the face and chest about a million times. It's like he doesn't want them to be recognized. Then he strips the body, moves it to a new location, and covers it up. From the looks of this one, she'd been dead about ten days before we found her. Her family reported her missing on the Fourth of July." He settles himself back in the seat. "You staying over tonight?" he asks.

"Right. I'll do some interviewing before I go back."

"Anything I can do to help, you let me know."

He understands the politics here; Kevin's is not the responding agency, and his plate is full. A serial murder case is one that can cost a person his job. Especially if it doesn't get solved quickly. This one has been going on too long. He imagines Kevin's department is developing a siege mentality, and this is a *pro forma* offer if he's ever heard one.

The secretary's house sits across the street from a large, tree-lined park. The front door opens and a tall, well-dressed young woman beckons them inside.

"Mrs. Ransome?"

"I'm her daughter." Turning to indicate the young man behind her. "This is my brother." *No names, please.* But the solidarity is good, he likes it.

They follow the two inside, where an older

woman sits alone on a couch. Her dark hair is cut short; her eyes are red from weeping. She wears a short-sleeved white blouse and black cotton skirt. She stands up to greet them, and her hand in Hugh's feels damp. She looks very nervous. He senses she could start crying again at the least provocation.

The daughter sits beside her mother, and her brother takes up a position behind the couch.

"I knew when you walked in the door this morning," Anne Ransome says to Kevin. "I knew from the first day. He's never gone away that long without phoning, not in all the years I've worked for him."

"How long is that?" Hugh asks, taking out pen and notebook.

"Twenty years. Edward and I go back a long time . . ." Her hand comes out of her skirt pocket, clutching a tissue. She wipes her eyes, blows her nose. The young man pats his mother's shoulder gently. "I have to get this said," she murmurs. "Something happened recently at the company. Something concerning the finances. Mr. Norbois found out in June there was money missing. And that the payroll taxes hadn't been paid for eighteen months. I knew about it back in January, when we first got the call from the state. But the comptroller kept telling Edward that he'd paid them, that it was a mistake, he had the canceled checks in the safe to prove it. I didn't believe it, not for one minute."

"Did you talk with Mr. Norbois about this?" Hugh asks.

"Oh yes." She stops to wipe her eyes. "I used to keep the books. But then Edward hired Roger Frisch—he's the comptroller—and as soon as he came here he started changing everything around. *Modernizing* he called it." Her voice takes on a bitter twist. "It was more like arranging things so nobody could tell what was going on but him. Edward said he came with excellent credentials, but I know how things like that can be fixed . . . and then I started worrying about the federal taxes, had they been paid? So I began doing some checking . . ." She takes a deep breath, reaching for the half-filled glass of iced tea sitting on the coffee table. "I went through the safe one day. I found out there weren't any canceled checks—for either the state or federal."

"And you told Mr. Norbois?"

"Of course. And of course Mr. Frisch tried to lie his way out of it. The auditors had given us a clean bill of health in April, there was nothing to worry about, he said." Again, the bitter tone has crept into her voice.

"When was this?" Hugh asks.

"About a month ago. Fortunately Edward had already talked to the IRS and so he had the facts in front of him. I should have figured it out sooner. According to the books, we were doing so well. Edward was talking about buying another small press in Ypsilanti . . . and then on June twenty-fifth—I remember because it was the day before they were supposed to leave for Banff—Edward called the office. I could tell he was furious. He asked to talk to Mr. Frisch. I knew there was something else wrong . . ." She sits a moment in silence, looking down at her hands. Her face is bright red. ". . . so I went into his office and listened in on the extension. I've never done anything like that before in my life! But I just had to know."

"What were they talking about?" Hugh asks.

"There was money missing. Hundreds of thousands of dollars . . . and Edward had found out about it somehow. He told Frisch he had three weeks to put it back. Frisch kept denying it . . . and Edward was so mad! I've never heard him talk like that to anybody . . . and right after that Mr. Frisch left the office. I didn't see him for the rest of the day."

"You say that was on the twenty-fifth? About what time?"

"Early. He was gone by ten, I'd say." Again, she shakes her head. "He pretends like it never happened, like it was just a business discussion they were having. But I know better . . . and now he has completely taken over. The rest of us report for work and do what he tells us to do. 'In the absence of Mr. Norbois, we'll be handling things *this* way.'" She looks up sharply. "I really believe he thinks this whole thing is going to blow over! Is he insane? That's obviously not going to happen!"

"Mom." The young woman rests a quieting hand on her mother's knee.

"So the whole family was leaving for Banff the morning of June twenty-sixth?"

"Yes. Edward faxed me the itinerary. And I expected to hear from him no later than the following Monday."

"And when you didn't hear, what did you do?"

"I called the airport in Pellston. They told me the plane was still there. I thought maybe Edward had decided to drive instead, although why they'd do that, I couldn't imagine. He'd filed a flight plan . . ." Her voice trembles and breaks, and she reaches again for the tissue, burying her face in it. Any control she'd been saving for this conversation is suddenly used up. She leans back against the couch, eyes closed, tears running down her face.

"Edward's been so good to me . . . my family, my children. I didn't have a penny to my name when he hired me . . . my husband left us when the kids were babies . . ."

"Ssh, Mom . . . it's okay," the young woman cuts her off, and her brother comes quickly around the couch. *No need to air all the dirty laundry here.*

"I should have called sooner." Her voice trembles. "I should have reported it to the police the minute I suspected."

"You did fine," Hugh says. "You called me."

"Yes, but I wasn't forceful enough! And I didn't do anything about it! I should have driven up there myself!"

Hugh stands up and pockets his notebook and pen. Both he and Kevin move toward the door. "We'll talk again soon, Mrs. Ransome," he says. "I don't believe there's anything more you could have done. They were already gone."

She looks at him, and this time her voice is calm. "I just want the truth to come out about this."

The sun is burning low in the sky; it hits their eyes, makes them both squint as they walk out to the patrol car.

"Well? She sure doesn't have a good word to say about old Rog, does she?" Kevin says. "I'm betting she's right on this one. You could get lucky."

"I'll talk to Frisch," Hugh says. "Get his take on this." He looks over at his friend. "I may need to use a few of your guys later on. For some interviewing."

"Yeah, sure. Call me later and we'll set it up. I'll have to fit them in, but I'll do what I can."

And Hugh doesn't blame him for this either; protecting his staff. They are on overload, too. Kevin is looking at his watch as they pull up in front of the station house.

"Take care, Hughie," he says as he climbs out of the car. A second later he is swinging off across the parking lot. *And that's that.* He is on his own in this one. His case is a blip on Kevin's radar screen; it will have to wait its turn.

LIES AND
DOCUMENTATION

THE OFFICES OF Challenge Press are tucked between Quick's Sandwich Shop and the St. Vincent de Paul Center, at the warehouse end of Division Street. The building's exterior is modest, if nondescript; not the kind of place ever to be targeted by the Historic Preservation Committee. Yet inside, the carpeting is a tasteful dark tweed, the wood-paneled walls are polished to a classic shine. The quarried tile throughout the building is original, Roger Frisch informs him as they approach his office.

A handsome man, thin and blond, with a small mustache and an air of the English gentleman about him, Frisch seems unfazed by Hugh's surprise visit this morning. It's hard to pin down his age; he could be fifty, Hugh guesses. Right now the pale blue eyes look dull, and the skin around them is tight with weariness.

"We're in a state of shock here," Frisch says. "As you may imagine. Still, there's work that has to be done."

A young woman passes them in the hall, wearing khaki shorts, a T-shirt that reads: "The Universe Rearranges Itself to Accommodate My Reality."

"Is the meeting still on, Mr. Frisch?"

"This afternoon? Yes. Have your presentation ready."

"It's ready." She's staring pointedly at Hugh's uniform, as if trying to puzzle out its meaning. "You'll be there, then?"

"Absolutely," says Frisch. "I'll handle whatever comes up. Don't worry."

She heads on down the hall, and Frisch raises his eyebrows at Hugh with a small smile. "I'm playing nursemaid these days. We have some creative types who aren't used to this kind of stress. Unless it's job-related, of course."

"I'd say most types aren't used to it," Hugh says.

Frisch opens the door to his office, indicates a chair near the desk. Hugh takes out his pen and notebook.

"How long have you worked for Edward Norbois?" he asks.

"I've been here a little over three years. I've loosened things up a bit, as you can see. Edward used to run a pretty tight ship before that."

"You were responsible for the day-to-day running of the business?"

Frisch shrugs his shoulders. "I wouldn't phrase it quite like that. Edward gave the orders. I simply carried them out."

"Were you worried when you didn't hear from him for so long?"

"No. I didn't expect to hear. We had things hammered out, and there wasn't any need for him to call. I figured they were just having a good time."

"But you were aware of Mrs. Ransome's concerns?"

Frisch shrugs. "Anne was Edward's secretary, not mine. She occasionally did things for me." A faint, dry smile. "Usually only when she had to, though. She's made no secret of how she felt about me from the beginning."

"Mrs. Ransome said you and Edward Norbois had an argument over the telephone. On the twenty-fifth of June."

For a moment Frisch looks truly puzzled. Then he frowns. "Not an argument, exactly. More a difference of opinion. I may have put things a little forcefully . . . she told you about that?"

"According to the phone records, it was a forty-three-minute call. It originated from Blessed. In Emmet County."

"Yes. I remember it. But we weren't arguing. We were discussing a client who owed us money. I had suggested that we get more serious about our collections. Edward refused. He got extremely frustrated during the conversation because I didn't agree with the position he was taking." He stops a moment, appears to be choosing his words carefully. "Anne Ransome is not someone who . . . she has been watching her power base erode here over the last three years. She isn't particularly pleased with the division of labor. Before I came, you see, she ran the show." He clears his throat. "She isn't exactly unbiased where I'm concerned. I don't mean to exaggerate this, but she's been with Edward a long time and these last months have been hard going for her. Plus, this mess over the payroll taxes hasn't helped things. But it's ridiculous. The state is insisting on something they absolutely cannot prove. If there's missing paperwork, it's not our fault. I'm sure it will all get straightened out eventually."

"Mrs. Ransome seems to think it's more than just missing paperwork."

"Yes, I know. But the auditors gave us a clean bill . . ." He sighs, and there is just the faintest flag of criticism.

Hugh shifts position in the chair. *Her exact words: a clean bill of health . . .* "Do you recall leaving the office after you took that phone call?"

"On the twenty-fifth of June?" Frisch riffles through his desk calendar. "Yes, sure. Here it is. Tri-State Alternative Press Convention. I went down to Cobo Hall in Detroit. The convention began early that morning. I left here around ten and spent the rest of the day there. Are you saying the twenty-fifth was the day of the murders?"

"The family was due to leave Blessed the next day. But the plane never took off. We're checking to see who might have seen or talked to them last."

Frisch ponders this a moment. "You aren't saying I could be a suspect in this? I mean, that's totally absurd!"

"We're still in the preliminary stages here," says Hugh. "I've got no idea who's a suspect and who's not."

"Yes, of course. I understand. It's such a terrible loss to all of us. And to the community at large . . ." Frisch clears his throat. "I've spoken to the surviving family members. It seems there are only three of them. They all live out of state. And I've also talked with Edward's attorneys. They told me the estate will take care of the funeral services as soon as the bodies are released. You wouldn't know when that might be?"

Hugh shakes his head. He jots down Billy Shaw's office number at Blodgett Hospital and hands it over to Frisch.

"The attorneys will need to file for the release of the bodies to persons other than family. After the autopsies are performed."

"Autopsies," echoes Frisch. "Yes, of course."

"One other thing," Hugh says. "I've contacted the forensic accountants, Miller and Webster. They'll be coming in to examine the books."

"This whole thing is so appalling," Frisch says. "I just hope it doesn't prove fatal to the company. A lot of jobs are dependent upon this firm's good name. I'd like to save them, if I could."

Lofty goals from a suspected embezzler. How reliable a witness is Anne Ransome? Hugh isn't as certain of her position as he was last night. What if Frisch is telling the truth? Why go to all this trouble if you know you are about to be caught in a lie? Either he embezzled the money, or he didn't. And if he did he'd better have a damned good alibi.

Yet he knows from past experience how innocent people can get swept up in murder investigations. Sometimes they do stupid things, too; like lying about facts that can be verified. That goes for both the quick *and* the dead.

———

"What can I say about them? They were wonderful people." Elaine Spiteri wipes her eyes. "We've been next-door neighbors for ten years. Since our twins were born. Paige's garden is the showplace of the neighborhood. She was a Master Gardener, you know . . . and Derek used to be our baby-sitter. He was the best-natured kid you'd ever want to meet."

She halts her monologue to glare across the coffee table at Hugh. Petite and blond, wearing tight black slacks and a sleeveless sweater, her long nails perfectly manicured. Her skin is darkly tanned; no sunscreen here. Her lips, painted bright pink, look almost fluorescent.

Hugh glances up at the cathedral ceiling soaring high above him. Everything is so bright in here; everything painted white. He finds himself squinting in order to see things more clearly.

Elaine Spiteri's husband Matt sits beside her. Younger than his wife by a few years, he looks like someone out of a Bally Fitness ad. He is also glaring at Hugh, as if he holds him responsible for this calamity.

"How in hell does something like this happen?

Some crazy person wanders in and does away with six people?"

Hugh resists the urge to clarify. *Does away with* wouldn't exactly be his choice of words. Something a little more graphic.

Elaine Spiteri reaches out to rest one hand on her husband's knee. "Honey, let the man talk." And then to Hugh: "What is it that you want to know?"

"Whatever you can tell me about them. As a couple, as a family. We're looking to fill in some blanks."

Elaine shrugs. "Edward owns an advertising agency and a publishing house. He publishes books mostly about landscaping and art."

"What was he like as a person?"

"Pretty much of a loner," Matt Spiteri says. "Not the friendliest guy you ever met."

"But Paige was great," says Elaine. "Very outgoing, very involved in community activities. She was president of the Women's Golf League here in the subdivision for a couple of years. That was before they bought the cabin. Since then they've spent most of their time up north. At least in the summers."

"Who were their closest friends?"

Elaine hesitates. "That would be us, probably. Me, really. Edward and Matt didn't have a lot in common."

"He wasn't the type you'd watch a football

game with on a Saturday afternoon," Matt says. "He didn't have many hobbies, other than flying his plane and working."

"Do you two have a key to their house?" Hugh asks.

"Yes," says Elaine.

"No," says Matt, then looks at his wife. "I mean, we did have one. But I gave it back. One time when Paige was locked out and couldn't find hers."

"I don't remember that," Elaine says. "Let me go and check." She leaves the room and returns in a few moments. "Yes. It isn't where I usually keep it. I guess that's right."

"Did you hear from them after they went up north?"

Both shake their heads no. "They went on a lot of vacations," Elaine says. "I actually thought they were in Canada."

"And Derek used to be your baby-sitter?"

"Yes. Before he left for college."

"Where did he go?"

"The University of Michigan. Where his dad went." Matt smirks. "It was ordained."

Elaine gives her husband a look.

"What about the younger kids?" Hugh asks.

"Davey and Nicole go to . . . went to private school," Elaine says. "Stephen was at Ann Arbor High."

"Did the kids have friends?"

"Sure," Elaine says. "The older boys—I'd see their friends' cars in the driveway all the time. When Derek graduated he had a party. They took pictures out on the lawn . . ."

"What are you driving at?" Matt asks.

"Nothing," says Hugh. "Just trying to get a sense of who they were."

"They were a normal family," he says. "Like everybody else."

"Their house was the showplace of the neighborhood," Elaine says. "Paige did all of it herself. She could've been a decorator." Again she clutches at her handkerchief as her eyes get teary.

"They got along okay with the other neighbors?"

"They didn't really hang out too much," Elaine says reluctantly. "Emil and Julie King— they're the party-givers and we've all been to their house. Paige and Edward only came once in a while."

"Paige chaired the school carnival with Kendra Jennings last year."

They list several other neighbors as Hugh writes them down. ". . . and there's Lizzy Trout— she was Nicole's best friend . . ."

Nicole. Hugh has forgotten the little girl for the moment. The image of the black-and-white sunsuit suddenly fills his mind. The blond braids.

The huddled figure. Resolutely he shoves the picture aside, rising and closing his notebook.

"Thanks for your time. I appreciate it."

Matt Spiteri walks him to the door. "Let us know if there's anything else we can do."

Evidently he has been forgiven for bringing bad news into Ann Arbor Estates. *No, not fair. Not their fault they live in cocooned splendor; not their fault their house boasts a cathedral ceiling.* But he does blame them for believing the mistake lies in straying from the haven of safety. These kids he sees playing tag outside are no different from any of the ones Hugh knows in Blessed. He wants to warn these people. *The world is a dangerous place. And bad things happen when you least expect them. So don't get too cocky. And don't relax your attention for even a single second.*

SIFTING THROUGH CHAFF

HUGH LETS HIMSELF into the Norbois house in Ann Arbor with the keys he found at the Blessed cabin. It feels cool and lifeless. Would this be true even if he didn't know what he knows about the owners?

On the grand piano is an array of family pictures: two older boys—these must be Derek and Stephen—at the beach with their kayak. A much younger boy in a blue wing chair, with a gold crown on his head proclaiming DAVEY IS TWELVE. And a little girl in ballet slippers and a filmy white tutu, a cap of white feathers encircling her head. *Nicole.*

There are many more, but his eye is caught by the color portrait of Edward and Paige with their children. Taken recently, he thinks; the ages of the four kids look about right. The background is that of a shady glen. The shot is posed and formal, telling its own story: Nicole, leaning against her father's arm, her hand on his shoulder; David, knees up and ankles crossed, seated in the grass at his mother's feet; the two older boys, separated by their mother, both looking handsome and slightly bored. Wealthy beautiful people, accustomed to life treating them well.

Hugh studies the oldest boy's bemused look; he's staring off into the distance, as if something better than this posing has caught his attention.

His eye moves to Nicole. Lovely name for a lovely little girl. The hand on her father's shoulder is delicate and long-fingered, as in an eighteenth-century painting. Intelligent-looking, healthy—her eyes reflect this, and her color is vibrant. Her blond hair is thick and luminous. Was she a good card player? A musician? A daddy's girl? *All meaningless now.*

Against his will, his mind leaps to Becky. His own little girl, his darling. What does he know about this horse camp she's going to? Is it safe? Are the counselors smart enough? Gentle enough?

Do they even know what they're doing, this bunch of college kids, new to the camp each year, and put in charge of the parents' most cherished possessions?

He turns away, walking across the wide living room to look out the window, and immediately he recognizes the setting in the picture: the same row of dark evergreens, the same manicured lawns. Somebody must be cutting the grass for them while they're away. A yard this large would require a lawn service. He believes this about photographs—that you can glean a world of personal information from them by studying the expressions and postures of the people. He also believes you can take this game too far.

Upstairs in the master bedroom everything is bathed in low light; the shades have been pulled as protection against the sun. It's too feminine for his taste: the crisp frilly white bedspread, the blue of the flowered drapes exactly matching the blue of the carpeting. Straight out of a decorating magazine.

He opens the nightstand drawer, finds what he was looking for—an address book. Expensive, fine-grained brown leather, with gilt trim around the edges. Paige Norbois is a very organized woman. *Was*. It's hard to think of her in the past tense. He notes how carefully each name is recorded with a black fine-tip pen; any changes

are annotated in green. Before each name is a date
of entry, with no names crossed out—merely a small
d., followed by a date. The two grandmothers—
Pearl Norbois, d. 1/15/2000; Elizabeth Worley,
d. 7/26/1989. And Clinton Norbois, Palm Beach,
Florida, d. 9/9/1995. Evidently Elizabeth Worley's
husband left the scene before the book was purchased. He pockets it and shuts the drawer.

The room next door is more to his liking;
David Norbois's seventh-grade homeroom picture is taped to the dresser mirror. The covers are
tossed across the foot of the bed and clothes are
strewn about the floor. The dresser is piled high
with video games and comic books. Hugh has to
smile; so like a kid to go away for the summer and
leave his bed unmade.

Nicole's, done in pastel plaid, is much like her
parents' bedroom—tidy and feminine. Ruffles on
the hem of the bedspread, curtains made of some
sheer fabric and tied back with ribbons. Nothing
out of place here; nothing to stop for, either. He
moves on to the room across the hall, where a
banner over the bed proclaims: STEPHEN CHASE
NORBOIS RULES. Messy, like David's, with the bed
barely made—a blanket carelessly pulled up over
the sheet and pillow.

A number of wallet-size photos are stuck into
the frame of the mirror—blond, smooth-featured

young women, all looking enough alike to be sisters. Hugh selects one, turns the photo over:

> Dear Stevie,
> You are cool and I
> Wish I'd gotten to know
> you better during this
> year! Chem was cosmic!
> Have a great senior year.
> Try to live happily ever after
> without me! (I know it'll be a
> struggle)
>   Your friend always,
>   Shelley Grand

He puts it back, takes up another:

> Steveboy,
> Never in a million years would
> I have picked you for a fellow
> Ben & Jerry's addict! Thanks for
> Skipping w/me—and for not tell-
> ing my secrets. Youse is a good
> kid. And—you are funny!
>   Tracy Kincaid

Feeling suddenly like an old man he slips the picture back into its place in the frame. This is like rolling back the clock and seeing them all with their lives still ahead of them. That confident, royal mien in the downstairs portrait. The clothes tossed over chairs, shoes in a heap on the floor, schoolbooks on the desk. Take it down, pack it away, haul it to the dumpster. All of it is junk now.

A wave of anger hits him and he turns away, heading farther down the hall. This last room is neat and orderly, with pewter walls and pale, woven throw rugs covering the dark burnished wood floor. The furniture is clean-lined and utilitarian. Here the artist of the family resides. On the walls are his pictures—watercolors, pen and pencil drawings, caricatures done in purple crayon—all signed with a carelessly scrawled *DN*. On the bed more sketches have been laid out, as if for a private showing. Hugh moves to look them over.

Most are merely line drawings, but one is a charcoal rendering of the photograph on the piano. He recognizes each of the faces, but something has been added—a casual, earthy look that erases the aloofness of the photograph. Here is the family as they really were. No doubt about it. An amazing knowledge of faces. This kid was an artist.

He sets the pictures aside. The house's silence suddenly oppresses him and he turns away, heading down the stairway to the front door. He pauses for an instant between the lifeless air inside and the oppressive heat behind the door. Then he steps into the late morning sun, pulling the door shut behind him; it closes with a merciless click. No sense in mourning now; these people were killed weeks ago. And whoever did the crime took pains to see that it wouldn't be discovered, taping that piece of cardboard over the bullet holes, pulling the drapes tightly closed, locking all the doors. Leaving nothing to arouse suspicion. Mourning isn't going to help solve it; thinking is what will solve it. He's a damned good thinker. And he'll find this guy, if it fucking kills him.

———

The article on the front page of the *Free Press* says it all: A TOWN HELD HOSTAGE. *Amid lush, pastoral beauty . . . a gruesome discovery . . . the model family . . . no known enemies . . . evidence meager and deteriorated . . . caretaker discovered bodies . . . Emmet County Sheriff Hugh DeWitt unavailable for comment.*

Great. Makes him sound like he was on vacation. He'd like to find out who it was who said that the evidence was "meager and deteriorated." It had better not be Ian.

He turns the page, finds that he's not the only one on the hot seat today. A double spread of the

Ann Arbor serial murders, with pictures of the victims: Valerie Dennis. Jane Peterson. Camilla Reusse. Sue Levin.

He studies the young women—all brunettes, all good-looking girls in their early twenties. All college students. Valerie Dennis, twenty-one, second-year nursing school, left her apartment September 25 to walk her dog. When the dog returned without her, Valerie's roommate called Ann Arbor police. Her nude body was found one month later under a pile of rocks in a farmer's field outside the town of Chelsea.

The second victim, Jane Peterson, a twenty-year-old art student, was reported missing by her roommate the evening of December 11, when she failed to return home from her waitressing job at Hazlitt's restaurant in Ann Arbor. Her car was found on the upper level of the State Street parking garage and, three weeks later, construction workers discovered her body stuffed in a storm drain off Earhart Road.

On March 15, Camilla Reusse disappeared after attending a late-night beer party in Delhi Park. On April 29 her nude body, wrapped in plastic, was found under a hedge in the arboretum. Police determined it had been stored somewhere else, then dumped in a sheltered corner of the preserve. The grass had been trampled from the nearby service drive all the way to the site.

The body had been eviscerated. She was by far the prettiest of the four women, with long, dark hair and high cheekbones, a delicate, patrician nose, and full lips. A look of intelligence about the eyes.

The mutilated corpse of Sue Levin was found just ten days ago. A second-year law student, living in Ann Arbor for the summer; reported missing July 4 by her parents, when she failed to show up for a family party in Muskegon. The body was found in a deserted farmhouse outside Ann Arbor.

This perp is getting sloppy. Less than two weeks between the murder and the discovery. Maybe he's running out of places to hide the bodies. Or maybe he's trying to get caught. That would be a break for Kevin. But Hugh doesn't believe it.

He tears out his article and pockets it, checks his watch. Nothing more to do here. If he leaves right now he can get back to Blessed by four o'clock.

MULTIPLE V. SERIAL

SEVERAL CARS ARE parked along the roadway of 119 near the Norbois cabin, and the highway patrol is directing traffic. Hugh turns in and drives to the top of the hill. He parks next to Terry Carlisle's green pickup. It has carried its share of bodies over the years. Six long metal boxes with web strapping are piled into the back end.

Harry Rose looks up as Hugh enters, gives him a curt nod. The room, cluttered with evidence paraphernalia, is a mess, but he knows that Harry is squarely on top of things. He is a good man, a good evidence tech, and he's lucky to have him. Three of the bodies on the floor now have sheets of black plastic over them.

Harry gestures with his thumb: *Let's get out of here.*

They exit the house and walk up the hill at the back. Harry pulls off his mask, clearing his throat and spitting into the nearby bushes. His eyes look sunken, his manner that of a man weary to the bone.

"Jesus, I'll be glad when this day is over." He lights a cigarette, blows out the match and drops it into the pocket of his overalls. "I told Terry he could start loading the bodies in an hour. We'll be ready to pack up around six."

This is not their first time together for this; over the years he and Harry have worked a lot of cases. Old men, living alone in shacks on property they've owned for a zillion years, their deaths going unreported; then a few utility payments are missed, or a neighbor reports a lack of activity. Or worse, much worse; kids playing with guns, a careless moment, a fatal accident.

"Did Doc DeVere sign the death certificates?" Hugh asks.

"Yeah."

"What about the photographs?"

"They're all up at your office." Harry takes a

long, deep drag, filling his lungs with smoke. Hugh pulls his handkerchief from his back pocket. Even a hundred yards away, the smell is still unbearable. *A dirty job, but somebody's got to do it.* One true meaning of that cliché.

"You were right," Harry says. "Bullets look like .32 caliber. Hollow point. All shots to the chest or the back, followed by one to the head. The ones that came through the window probably killed the man instantly. Both of them smack into the heart."

"How many shots altogether?"

"Eleven, maybe twelve. They shot everybody but the little girl. They beat her head in with some kind of blunt instrument. Then they stabbed her. Then somebody went back and stabbed the mother for good measure. Guess they wanted to make sure everybody was good and dead."

"Find any casings?"

"Not a one. Couple of slugs in the floor, one in the chair, one in the wall behind the table. But they won't be worth much. Too badly damaged. Likewise the ones in the bodies."

"Murder-suicide not an option, I take it."

Harry barks a laugh. "Not unless you can figure how somebody shoots himself from six feet away and then blows his brains out." He takes a long drag on his cigarette. "There's more," he says. "Looks like both the woman and the little girl were raped. It's hard to tell for sure at this point, could be lacerations in the genital area, could be splitting from general pressure buildup. But along with the positioning of the bodies that's what I'm guessing."

Damn hell son of a bitch. Hugh doesn't want this to be a sex crime, doesn't want that added to the mix, it's too much.

He and Harry head back to the cabin and he replaces the mask dangling at his neck. Just outside the back door he glances down at a large rock off to the side of the path. A pile of tiny beads are assembled there, along with a piece of fine string. He bends down to look more closely. No, it's snail shells. A bracelet. Someone was in the process of making a bracelet.

He clears his throat and stands up. Harry is holding the door for him.

"You sending Ian down with the truck?"

Hugh nods. The first rule of police procedure: The chain of evidence must not be broken.

Ian is coming down the stairway. "Glad you're here, Hugh. It's a zoo. There's a shitload of reporters, all trying to get over on each other. Plus Coby's crazy wife is trying to break him out."

"Tell Emma she can come pick him up around six. That'll give me time to give him a talking to. I want you to follow the bodies down to Grand Rapids. Take somebody with you. Then you and

he can keep on going to Ann Arbor. There are
some people down there I want you to talk to."
Hugh reaches into his back pocket, pulls out the
brown leather address book. "I found this at the
house. I've gone through it and marked the ones
I want you to call."

"What's with the Ann Arbor police? They
aren't working this one with us?"

"They want to be kept informed."

Ian rolls his eyes. "Yeah, well . . . They've got
four bodies, we only have six. Makes sense to me.
Multiple versus serial, huh?"

"Where'd you get that?"

"Saw it on an old *Dragnet* episode."

"You're watching too much TV. Tell Terry not
to try to break any speed records, okay? Make
sure that tarp gets fastened down tight."

He enters the office and Fredda looks up in relief:
a half-dozen reporters are standing at the counter,
vying for her attention. They all move as one in
Hugh's direction:

"Sheriff, you looking to charge anybody in this
crime?"

"You mean right now? No."

"We heard you've already got somebody in
custody."

"*Protective* custody. Not the same thing."

"Is it the caretaker you think is involved?"

"The caretaker found the bodies, that's all, guys."

"You thinking of setting up a special hotline?" someone asks. "They've got one going for the coed killings downstate."

"No plans at this time," Hugh says, walking purposefully toward his office. He calls to Fredda: "*You.* I need to see you in my office. *Pronto.*"

He can't seem to help it, he always starts talking like a hick country sheriff the minute any strangers show up. Something about the way they look at him. Or does he view himself that way? Fredda dutifully closes the office door behind her.

"*Pronto?*"

"Sorry about that." He forces himself to smile. "Listen, I need to talk to Coby right now. Tell those guys I'll be back to see them a little later."

She frowns. "They're okay. Just give them a little of your attention. They need somebody to tell them what to think."

"All right."

"There's a television crew coming in tomorrow. They want an interview at the site."

He sighs, taking the keys from his desk drawer. Walking through the back hallway to the holding tank, he looks through the window at Coby, lying comfortably on the daybed, flipping through a magazine. He unlocks the door.

"Where *you* been?" Coby accuses him.

"Out of town," Hugh says.

"What am I doin' in here, Hugh? All I said was I never did like the guy. That don't mean I killed him, for God's sake! I maybe overcharged him a little, that's all. Man's gotta eat, y'know. Gotta feed his family."

"You own a .32 semiautomatic, Coby?"

"Sure I do. Don't everybody? But I ain't fired the thing in a while. I'm not even sure I know where it is."

"That's the first rule of hunting," Hugh says. "You *always* know where your weapon is. Is it registered?"

"Of course it is. You think I'm some dumbass doesn't know enough to license his firearms?"

Coby's shoulders sag. Hugh sits down beside him.

"He was a dumb bastard, Hugh. Diggin' into the side of that hill . . . buildin' some cockeyed castle up there. Don't he see how it'll be the ruination of that piece of property?"

Coby's French ancestors were men who could hold their own with county landowners like the Charbonneaus, Bissonettes, and Gautiers. Now his family's wealth consists in a tiny plot of boulder-strewn property up near the river.

"No, he's got his own dumb plan and he don't listen to nobody," Coby goes on. "I say the guy got what he deserved."

"Don't be an asshole," Hugh says. "You think Norbois deserved this? You think his family deserved it? A ten-year-old girl deserves to be hit in the head until she dies? You're crazier than I thought, Coby. Someone does something so sick—right here in our county—and you're up at the Captain's Corner, trying to explain it so it makes sense."

Coby's head drops to his chest. "I didn't mean those kids," Coby mutters.

"They're dead all the same, though, aren't they?"

Coby coughs out a sob; tears spurt from his rheumy eyes. "Listen, my kid didn't deserve gettin' run over by no drunk SOB out on a huntin' trip, neither! My kid had a family, too! What good did it do him, I ask you?" He wipes a hand across his face. "What good did it do yours?"

Hugh's heart thumps eerily inside his chest. He doesn't want to trade losses with Coby LaChappelle, not here in the holding cell, not anywhere. "Go on home now," he says. "And quit trying to get your name in the papers."

FASHION SHOW

He ARRIVES HOME a little after seven and parks his car in the garage. Some reporters might decide they didn't get enough at the meeting and go cruising through town looking for him.

Karen hands him a glass of iced tea.

"I think I need something stronger. What's been happening around here?" He pulls out a kitchen chair and sits down, realizing suddenly that he is exhausted and that his muscles are stiff with tension. He stretches his arms over his head, yawning.

"Nothing much," she says.

He swallows the tea in three gulps, surprised at how good it tastes. She refills his glass as Becky enters the kitchen.

"This," she announces, "is for the gymkhana. When you and Mom come up to the ranch."

He takes in the jodhpurs, plaid shirt, and pale tan cowboy hat. "What's a gymkhana?"

"It's a horse show. Where you get to show off what they can do. Don't you remember from last year, Daddy?"

He is so happy to see them both, so full of gratitude for that which is his, and, of course, this sudden rush of love plunges him predictably into despair. But despair is not the right mood for a fashion show. And Becky won't hear of it, in any case. She is off again, returning almost instantly in a new outfit: a dress, made of some slippery material and ending just above her knees.

"What do you think?"

"I think," he says, "that you look like a teenager. Hey, Beck, you're not gonna grow up on me now, are you?"

"Jenny Wold's parents want to talk to you guys," Becky says. "They're getting nervous about her going away."

"Hasn't she been to camp?" Karen asks.

"No. I told them there was nothing to be worried about."

"The first time is scary," Hugh says. "For the parents, I mean."

"I guess so."

"So, what's the deal? Is everybody wearing clothes three sizes too small for them these days?"

She smiles at him with infinite patience, rooted in the genes she carries, along with those of her mother.

"I knew you wouldn't get it," she says, twirling on her toes in front of him. The telephone rings and Karen goes to answer it.

"Hello? Yes he is, just a minute." She hands him the receiver with a questioning look.

"Sheriff DeWitt? It's Elaine Spiteri. I thought I should tell you something. I didn't mention it when you were here this morning." A long pause. "It's about Paige."

"Yes?" He smiles at Becky as she reappears, wearing a two-piece swimsuit, then turns to Karen to raise his silent objection: *What is this, Club Med?*

"She was having an affair," says Elaine Spiteri. "With someone I know. As a matter of fact, I introduced them to each other. Of course he's got nothing to do with this, but I thought you should have all the facts."

"Who is it?"

"His name's James Faber. He's a stockbroker. He's with a firm here in town."

"I appreciate your telling me," Hugh says. "It's important that we contact as many people as we can."

"Well, that's what I thought. He could have some information." And then, a moment later: "Oh, that won't be necessary. If I decide to go ahead with it, I'll give you a call. Thanks so much." And she is gone. He hangs up.

"That was weird."

"Somebody about the case?" Karen asks.

"Somebody who didn't want anyone else to know who she was talking to."

He lies on his back in bed, hands under his head, waiting for Karen. He could fall asleep right here if he's not careful. But he doesn't want to do that, wants to stay awake tonight. Too many nights of not talking to her makes him feel detached; he needs to stay centered in his own life. This world of quiet normalcy that she and Becky inhabit— eating meals, buying clothes, making plans—is what he misses most when he's on a case; he needs that for balance.

"What happened in Ann Arbor?" she asks as soon as she slips into bed.

"Not much. I talked to the secretary. And this morning I saw the comptroller and the next-door neighbors. What I get is that they were a close-knit family. And the guy was a workaholic. Somewhat impatient with the failings of the world. A shoot-from-the-hip-type guy."

"How old were the kids?" she asks. "Tell me their names."

"Derek, the oldest, was nineteen; Stephen was seventeen, David thirteen, and Nicole ten."

She is silent a moment. "People in town are leaning toward the homicidal maniac theory."

"I don't buy that. That's just some nightmare fiction to scare the kids with." He rolls over to stare at the wall. "Here's another puzzle. Nobody I've talked to so far, with the exception of the secretary, has expressed concern or surprise about how long these people were out of touch. Didn't they have anybody who kept track of them? Didn't anyone miss them? This strikes me as odd."

"Not so odd, maybe. After all, their friends in Ann Arbor wouldn't expect to hear much. And they obviously didn't know many people up here."

"Yeah, but what about the kids? People they emailed on a regular basis. Any activities that might require them to communicate. They all seemed so isolated. I don't get it."

"Unless," Karen says, thinking out loud, "unless the person most apt to keep in touch is the murderer. Then, the longer the secret's kept, the better."

"The logical suspect is Roger Frisch. The company comptroller. He had a fight with Norbois over the phone the day of the murders. After which he leaves the office and isn't seen again."

"Sounds like a no-brainer," Karen says, yawning. "No-brainers do happen, Hugh."

"Yeah," Hugh says. "I know this sounds ridiculous. But he doesn't strike me as the type. So far, he's the only one with any kind of motive, the only one with something to gain. But why kill the whole family? Why not wait for some dark night to ambush Norbois and make it look like an accident? Or a robbery? And why so vicious? Why beat a ten-year-old over the head with a hammer and then rape her? What kind of a monster does something like that?"

"Was she raped?" Karen asks softly. "Oh, Hugh . . ."

"Yeah, and the wife, too."

She puts her arms around him and he lets out a weary sigh. It feels like he's been holding it in for a long time.

"I don't know if I'm going to be able to drive Beck up to camp," he says. "I may have to head down to Ann Arbor again. Stay there for a while. Get some more information."

"Don't worry about it," she says. She reaches

up to switch off the light. In the dark she turns to him, fitting her body into the hollow of his stomach, once again slipping her arms around him. He kisses her gently, feels an answering throb in the region of his groin. He slides his knee slowly, back and forth, between her legs.

"What's up?" she whispers. He doesn't answer her, simply moves in closer. But of course, just as he believes himself safe, the problem surfaces and he has been tricked again. A small groan escapes him, but Karen, still trying, holds him tighter about the waist and, sweating with effort, he submits, hoping to catch the rhythm from her, but it doesn't happen and he knows immediately that it won't, recognizes this all-too-familiar scenario. *Damn, damn, damn.* Holding himself against her as she stiffens and lets loose, he kisses her hair, then carefully moves to free himself.

"I thought it was working . . ." she murmurs.

"It was," he says. "As far as it went."

"You okay? You want anything?"

"Nope. D'you?"

"Sure," she says wistfully. "I want us to fuck our brains out and then go have a hot fudge sundae."

"You were the one feeding me iced tea," he says. "You know it takes a quart of scotch."

There's a pregnant silence. Then: "When are you going to see somebody about this, Hughie?"

"Oh, *fuck*."

"Don't get mad. It's just a *physical* thing . . ."

"It sure is." For some reason he finds this hilarious, and he laughs into his pillow. "Look, let's not talk about it right now. I promise I *will* go."

"When?"

"*Jesus!* I don't know. Soon."

"Because the men in those TV ads . . ."

"Oh, *please*. Nobody in his right mind would do an ad like that if he actually had a problem." To calm himself he bites her ear. "I swear I'll do it, Karey. Soon."

WISHFUL THINKING

Hugh dials Ian's pager and sits back in the chair in his office. He stares out at the cedars across the parking lot, tossing in the stifling hot wind.

"Hey. What's up?"

"Where are you?"

"Inside the rolling hills of Ann Arbor Estates. I took Stan West with me. He's on Bankers' Boulevard, I'm working Lawyers' Lane."

Hugh fills Ian in on Paige Norbois's lover. "Look him up in the address book, will you?"

"Hey, yeah, James Faber. He's here all right."

"Good. Take a trip over to his office. See what he's got to say."

"Looks like the median age in this subdivision is around seventy. With a couple of pockets of younger couples."

"When you get a chance," Hugh says, "check with the station house and see if either Derek or Stephen Norbois has a juvenile record."

"Will do. Hey, there's an ad in today's *Ann Arbor News*. Full page. A hundred-thousand-dollar reward for information leading to the arrest and conviction of the killer of Edward Norbois and his family. Offered by Challenge Press, Roger Frisch, Comptroller."

"Interesting."

"Plus, there's a citizens' committee raising money to hire a psychic. They want him to come here and examine the evidence surrounding the coed murders."

"Everybody wants to get into the cop business."

He hangs up, looking again at the record of people whose names caught his attention when he was leafing through the address book. He dials the number listed for Nell Messenger (piano teacher) and introduces himself.

"Oh. You're calling about Paige and Edward." The voice is so soft he can barely make it out. And again he's reminded of how much he hates these calls. Talking with friends or relatives of the deceased. Dealing with anger and grief, with fear and shock; donning the regulation disguise of the police professional.

"I still can't believe this," the woman whispers. "Did someone break in? Is that what happened?"

"We're not certain yet," he says. Again, the stock answer. What would this person do with the real information? What *is* the real information? *Don't worry, they didn't suffer.* How could he know this? He doesn't know this. Some of them surely suffered, but at least the suffering had an end. And what were those two kids thinking as they raced up the stairway toward the one chance they had? That had to have been the case: They were trying to get to the 30.06 rifle in the closet.

"I was hoping you could talk with me for a few minutes. About the Norbois family—"

"Oh no," she says. "I couldn't possibly. This is just too much. I'm sorry. No." Without another word she quietly hangs up. He sits holding the receiver as Fredda appears in the doorway.

"I heard you talking. Did she just hang up on you?"

"Yeah."

"Should I try to get her back?"

"No. I'll have Ian stop by."

"Chief Watkins is on line two."

"Thanks."

"Hugh," says Kevin, "the forensic accountants just called. They've been over at Challenge Press, going through the books and bank statements. They think they've found some checks that may have been forged. Made out to cash, supposedly signed by Edward Norbois, only they don't think it's his signature."

"What does Frisch say?"

"He hasn't been told. He called in sick today. Hang on just a sec, can you?" In the background he hears loud voices. In a moment Kevin returns. "Sorry about that. Jesus, you wouldn't believe it. I got another guy wants to 'fess up to the serial killings. Where do they slither out of, anyway? Don't know one damned thing about the case, don't even know the women's names, they just know they want to give it up and throw themselves on the mercy of the court."

"I heard about the citizens' committee from my deputy this morning," Hugh says.

Kevin snorts. "Yeah, the stupid cops can't solve these crimes, so let's go get somebody from outer space."

"Think they'll hire him?"

"Hell, it's been done. Some psychic from California is on his way here, even as we speak. Newspapers are having a field day. Listen, about Frisch—this guy has definitely messed with the books, the accountants say. I'm thinking you might want to get down here before he decides to take a trip. Aren't there a couple of your people in town? I thought I saw somebody in the office."

"Yes. Checking out the juvenile records of the Norbois kids."

"I doubt you'll need them. This guy's the doer for sure."

Thanks for the tip. He can't let this one go by. "Since when is writing bad checks in the same league with blowing six people away?"

"He was going to lose his job over it."

"Doesn't it strike you as an extreme reaction?"

"You gotta take your gift horses when you see 'em." A signoff, if ever he's heard one. *Expect no additional help from this end.*

Hugh calls Ian and gives him the information on the accountants' findings.

"What do you want Stan and me to do?"

"Just keep an eye on Roger Frisch. We wouldn't want to have to put out an APB on a guy who looks this guilty. And see if you can talk to the piano teacher. Nell Messenger."

"Okay. Will do."

Hugh hangs up and dials the Grayling State Police lab. Mack Gellar's secretary tries to palm him off on the deputy chief; he'll have none of that today.

"Tell him it's an emergency. Tell him I'll wait."

"What's up?" Gellar asks when he gets on. Testy, but Hugh is used to that.

"I'm sending over some spent bullets from the crime scene. I'm also ordering DNA tests from Blodgett Hospital," he says. "It looks like the two females were raped."

"You got a suspect yet?"

"Maybe. Not sure."

"Who do you like? Homicidal maniac or half-brained handyman?"

"Neither."

"Okay, then. Disgruntled employee. I talked to one of my guys yesterday. They say the smell over there is unbelievable. Too bad. The heirs are gonna have to torch the place."

Probably thinking about his turn-of-the-century farmhouse in Grayling. Funny how it's easier for some people to mourn a domicile than it is for them to grieve over the human beings inside.

The Norbois cabin looks grim and forbidding in the soupy fog—the aftermath of last night's rain. The cedar trees are dripping, still draped with yards of yellow police tape. The two deputies on duty wave as he drives up. No other vehicles; must be too early for the reporters. Even with the bodies gone, the air is still thick with the perfume of death.

He walks up the slate pathway toward the front door. Halfway there he stops, cutting across the spongy ground to the front window. The piece of cardboard is gone, taken away as evidence. He remembers when he first saw this spot; his impression was that it had been watered down and swept clean, no doubt in order to obliterate the footprints made by the murderer as he stood there and took aim.

All .32-caliber bullets, all looking as if they were fired from the same gun. He stands before the window, cocking his finger to pull back a trigger. He would have taken aim in just this spot, at this angle. And then what? Would he have made for the front door as fast as he could, in order to catch the rest of the family by surprise? Would he have checked first, making sure the door was unlocked? Or did he have some knowledge that it would be? Did he know these people, know their habits? How else could one person ever manage to pull this off? Hugh is convinced now that it was a single killer. He's not even sure why he knows this, but he does.

He looks down at the ground. The area has already been screened by magnets; he ordered it done yesterday. Yet the feeling persists that there is something else needing to be checked out. Kneeling, he runs his hands lightly over the soil in the spot where a shell casing would likely have been ejected. The killer was smart enough to take the rest of the casings with him; it follows then, that he would have retrieved the ones out here as well. But not right away. There wouldn't have been time. What if he couldn't find them later? What if, in the intensity of the moment, he forgot them? That doesn't appear to be the case, though.

He rises and enters the house through the front door, stepping around a shadowy stain outlined in yellow chalk. Moving to the stairway, he stops to study the arc of blood splashing up the wall. Someone was shot while running up these stairs. What if one of the brothers was trying to block the killer's path? Even a few seconds more could have made the difference, could have allowed the other one to reach the rifle in the closet.

The bedrooms are just as he remembered them—suitcases lying, partially packed, on several of the beds. In the smaller, front bedroom he notices something sticking out from beneath the bedclothes. He lifts the mattress and looks below. On the box spring lies a small bundle wrapped in a piece of cloth. He opens it. Inside is a deck of tarot cards. He recognizes them because Becky has a deck. She asked for them last Christmas. Now and then she does readings for Hugh and Karen. Madame Swami, he calls her. He shuffles through the cards, puts them back inside the cloth, folding the ends over neatly. It looks like a silk scarf. He sets the deck on the dresser.

In the room where the bodies had lain he notices that one of the beds is spread with a collection of sketches. More of Derek's work. Odd that in both houses he's seen drawings arranged in this fashion, as if someone had been studying them. He looks through the drawings, marveling again at the skill with which they've been executed. Here is a caricature of Derek's father on the beach, the dock in the background. He's reading a newspaper. The name of the periodical is carefully penned: *The Wall Street Journal*. Edward's hooded eyes are fixed on the page, his mouth set in a taut frown. Hard to imagine capturing this pose without the full consent of the sitter. Yet it seizes with such accuracy what little Hugh knows of the man's character—rigid, formal, humorless.

The remaining sketches—some watercolor, some pen and ink—are serious, detailed; a reflection of the artist's obsession with people. Drawings and sketches of faces and figures, all of them painstakingly done.

"Anything you need, sir?" Joe Iverson sticks his head around the corner of the bedroom.

"No, thanks. How's it going? Boring duty, huh?"

Joe nods. "Toughest part so far is keeping the paper boys away." A lanky, first-year deputy,

Iverson is a wise guy, usually with a collection of quips at the ready. This morning he seems subdued. "Kinda weird, isn't it? Them lying out here alone for all that time. Makes you feel sad." His face is smoothly composed, but the eyes look vulnerable. Surprised, Hugh nods his head. And just as quickly, the moment is past. What else is there to be said? They both turn away, heading for the stairs.

Thumbtacked to a wall in the living room is a large laminated map of Lake Michigan with streaks of dark blood smeared across its surface. Hugh looks away, toward the front window and beyond, to the misty woods and the gravel parking area. A memory stirs. Of Ian and himself as they enter the room. Playing cards scattered over the floor. Putrid, decaying flesh. *Hugh . . . the stairway . . . look over here . . .* going upstairs to the bedroom, where the bodies are sprawled in front of the closet. Outside, the sound of a car door slamming. A glimpse from an upstairs window, of a flutter of blue cloth, a bristling, gingery mane. *Oh, Jesus.* That's why Coby was standing there beside the car. That's why his look was so morose, so determined.

TWO BROTHERS

THE YELLOW HOUSE on Medoc Road sits at an angle on the property, gray shutters nailed shut on the upper story, the roof thick with moss. The overhanging pines that shelter it from the sun provide the perfect medium for bacteria growth. Ten years ago they might have saved it. By now the decay is rampant. There have to be major leakage problems inside.

The rain has resumed, and Hugh parks the patrol car close to the house, on the sandy drive, hurries up the steps to the front door. He knows they are watching him. Normally he'd take it slow, giving them time to assess the situation. The LaChappelles are a wary, suspicious bunch. Their hand-lettered sign, brushed with tree paint on a piece of barn wood, is planted in the center of the yard:

THE BEST SOCIETY IS WHERE
EVERYONE'S EQUAL AND
NOBODY LIVES UPSTREAM

"Nobody" is the Banfields, who've staked a claim to the property east of Coby's, on the river. It would take one quick stop at the county clerk's office to clear up a misunderstanding that has endured for as long as Hugh can remember, but the two families have come to relish the feud. In the same way that Emma likes to get up a petition each spring to ban angle parking on Lake Street.

"Morning, Hugh."

Emma, in a rose-colored bathrobe, pushes the screen door open.

"Morning, Emma," Hugh says. "The boys around?"

"Harmon's still asleep."

The LaChappelle brothers, together with wives and children, lived here for years, until Harmon's wife died and all of the kids moved out; now these three are the only ones left at home. Coby, the younger of the two brothers, supports Harmon along with any and all wayward children and grandchildren. In the broad scheme of things, he is the responsible member of his clan.

"Coby's in the kitchen." Emma leads him through a hallway lined with cardboard boxes to the small room at the rear of the house. The rectangular sink, its U-joint exposed, looks sporty and primitive; a red-checked dishcloth is drying over the porcelain drainboard.

Angled across a corner is a Hoosier cupboard, painted dark red. A new side-by-side refrigerator/freezer sits opposite. Between them is a square of worn, cherry-red carpeting. This room is the center of activity in the household. Coby, seated at a table by the window, is reading the morning paper.

"Rain's really comin' down," he observes. "Like cows peein' on a flat rock. Munising gets all the good weather. Stops right at the bridge."

Hugh seats himself at the table, and Emma pours him a cup of coffee.

"Says right here we oughta be stockin' up on duck tape," Coby says. "Now how's that gonna save us? I ask." He leans back in his chair. "Back when I was a kid it used to be hay wire. Then it went to binder twine. Now it's duck tape."

Hugh laughs and Coby smacks his hand down

on the table, signaling an end to the small talk. "Got somethin' on your mind, Sheriff DeWitt?"

So it's to be a formal conversation. "A couple of things, Coby. I'm wondering where you went after you left the Norbois's place the other day."

"Went straight to your office. Drove like a bat outta hell. Probably broke the speed limit. Gonna give me a ticket?"

"The second time," Hugh says. "When Ian and I were inside and you were supposed to wait for us in the car."

Silence. But Coby is a man who yearns to talk. The best approach is to wait it out.

"That was a bad day, Hugh."

"One of the worst."

"Doc DeVere says he never saw nothin' like it in his entire lifetime." Coby fixes his gaze on the iron stove in the center of the room. Mostly it provides heat in the winter, but sometimes there are meals made on it, even though a modern-day range is sitting next to the sink.

Hugh remembers the evening when this house was headquarters for a celebration of deputies and neighbors; when Emma made dozens of burgers on the old flat grill, and the beer flowed into the night. A cold day in November, after four-year-old Sylvie Banfield wandered off and disappeared into Tucker Marsh, and the desperate urgency to find her was spurred on by the rapidly falling temperatures. Hugh can still see the joy on Fred Banfield's face as his daughter was carried, unharmed, out of the cedar swamp in the arms of Harmon LaChappelle. It was Hugh's first year as sheriff.

"I didn't want to go back there that day, I told you," Coby says.

"What were you doing under the windows?" he asks.

"I didn't do nothin' wrong, Hugh."

"Coby, I think you did."

Another long silence. "It wasn't a fair deal," Coby says. "He fired Harmon for no reason. Didn't even speak to him in person, didn't have the nerve. Left it for the foreman." He stares out the window. "Harmon's ten times the finish carpenter they hired in his place. Steady as you get when he's not drinkin'."

Hugh nods. He waits for Coby to gather his thoughts.

"I asked Harmon if he done it," Coby says. "He told me *no*. That's enough for me."

"Fine. So now what's your plan? How're you going to fix it so I don't suspect either of you?"

"What d'you mean?"

"I mean where are the casings you picked up? I hope to God you kept them."

"I wasn't in my right mind that day, Hugh."

"That's a true statement. But you see the problem, don't you? Even if you kept them, how do I know they're the same ones you picked up? They could be any .32-caliber casings now, couldn't they?" He stops to let Coby plumb the depths of this. "You broke the chain of evidence when you picked them up. Now you're in it, and I'd say off-hand you're deeper in than your brother."

On cue, Harmon stands in the doorway wearing the dirty overalls and gray flannel undershirt that is his trademark. His boots are unlaced, his lank hair in disarray.

"So you called him. Good. Let's get this thing over with once and for all." Harmon shuffles across the room. "You look me in the face, Hugh DeWitt. You tell me I done this wicked cruel thing, just you go ahead."

"Nobody's saying that. I want to know what happened to the casings."

"Don't you go making a fool of yourself, Harm," says Coby. "You wasn't the one and everyone knows it."

"No, but *you* was the one fixed it so's it looks like I done it! I got *you* to thank for that!"

And now the beef is squarely between the brothers, where it has always been. Hugh shakes his head as Emma appears in the doorway. "You two, I'm takin' the truck over to Posen. Coby, stop actin' like an idjit and give them casings to Hugh."

With a sigh, the old man rises from his chair, walks straight to the shelf above the stove, and opens the box of kitchen matches.

"Ain't but one. I found it wedged under a juniper branch, half-buried in the dirt. I was gonna give it to you that day, but you were inside. And I couldn't go in there again, Hugh, not with all that . . ." Eyes on the floor. "You gonna charge me?"

"With what? Being an idiot?"

"Tamperin' with evidence . . ."

"I ought to. If I weren't an idiot myself, I would. Now both of you hand over your guns."

"Hugh, that shell never come from mine," Harmon whines. "I ain't even fired it since last fall."

"I don't give a damn," he says. "I want to see you both this afternoon over at Doc DeVere's. For blood samples. It's the quickest way to get you off the hook. And for God's sake, don't be noising it all over town. Stay away from the phone, that's all I ask."

"Listen," Coby says. "I think I seen the guy who did this."

"Coby, don't mess with me."

"No, I seen someone skulkin' around up there. Long before the bodies was found."

"What are you talking about?"

"Fourth of July weekend. I went up to check

on things and I spotted this guy. He was up by the driveway, and when he sees me he takes off . . ."

"What kind of car?"

"Didn't see no car. He was runnin' to beat hell off in the woods. I started chasin' him, but he had too good of a start on me. Young guy, he was . . ."

"What'd he look like?"

"Light-haired, kinda thin. Clothes looked like he might of been from the city. Wasn't from around here, I know that much. I shoulda mentioned it before . . ."

"Coby, you'd better not be lying to me—"

"Don't it make sense, though? I mean, the bodies was just layin' up there. Who'd be hangin' around if it wasn't the murderer, comin' back to visit the scene of the crime?"

Hugh collects their guns and heads for the door, and his last view is of the two of them standing under their rotting roof, a pair of forlorn wayfarers looking for all the world as if he has abandoned them.

DNA AND OTHER
DATA

GRAND RAPIDS IS growing. The city itself used
to cluster—Oz-like—within a realm of flat green
fields. No more. Now it ruthlessly pursues the
surrounding countryside, sprawling its way across
both sides of Highways 131 and I-96.

Standing before the windows in Billy Shaw's
office in Blodgett Hospital, Hugh gazes at the
downtown skyline, remembering a time when his
father nearly accepted a job here, in Police
Administration. He can't imagine how differently his and his brother's lives would have turned

out had this happened. Grand Rapids feels like a fractured place to him, with the strict religious values he associates with a more pastoral setting, and the seemingly relentless municipal construction.

"I'm leaning toward the single-shooter theory," Billy says. He is standing at his desk, a sheaf of papers in his hand. "What about you?"

"Yeah. That's what I think, too."

Billy's office is roomy and well furnished, hardly reflecting the business of the head of Forensic Pathology. It resembles the high-class digs of a professional photographer, with its cream-colored walls upon which are plastered dozens of prints of exotic settings around the world.

"Those over there are new," Billy points out. "I took them in Rwanda. At the gorilla sanctuary."

"Pretty impressive."

Billy laughs. "I always like showing you my stuff, Hughie. You know just what to say. Your guy Harry Rose is an ace, by the way. Where'd you pick him up?"

"MSU," Hugh says.

"Samples are as clean as any I've seen. As good as the stuff I get from Grayling. Good tissue means good serology."

"Always looking on the bright side," Hugh says. "Tell me what you think about the woman and the little girl."

"Severe tearing of the vaginal tissues. More than just normal decomposition would allow. I took DNA samples just in case. You got any for me? Any suspects yet?"

"That's the next order of business."

"You looking at RFLPs or PCRs?"

"Whichever's faster."

"PCR. By far. But it's got a big drawback. Fewer variants. I'd advise going with RFLP or both. You'll get better results."

"How long are we talking?"

"A month. Maybe more. Depending on what we're after. PCRs don't differ much from one lab to the next, but RFLPs will. Different labs use different binning strategies. That'll affect the time."

Billy would love to go on, but Hugh holds up his hand; he's already in over his head. Any more talk of probes, protocols, lengths of polymorphisms, and VNTRs, and the picture will just get muddier.

"When are you releasing the bodies?" Hugh asks.

"Today. I'll call the lawyers. Hey, I read the papers, too, you know. Is the business partner a suspect?"

Hugh smiles. "Don't count my chickens."

"Mr. James Faber," Ian says, when Hugh gets him on the phone. "This guy is good. He 'fesses up to the affair with the Mrs. right off the bat. Honest as the day is long. Wants to make a clean breast of it."

"Somebody gave him a heads-up."

"That's my guess. Or else he's just a very slick dude."

"Married?"

"Divorced. Says he and Paige Norbois recently stopped seeing each other. Her idea. He was waiting for her to think it through and reconsider. Evidently she's done it before, gotten to feeling guilty and broken things off."

"How's his alibi?"

"We're checking it out."

"What about the piano teacher? Did you get hold of her?"

"Nell Messenger. Oh, yeah. We went to the apartment and there she was, getting ready to take off in her car. Black Ford Mustang convertible, 5 point 0. Top down and all. She's about thirty-five, anorexic, and very, very nervous. Didn't want to talk about Mrs. Norbois, not her business, wouldn't have anything to contribute. All the time she's looking like she's expecting somebody to jump her from behind the bushes. She taught Nicole piano ever since she was five. Except not this year. I asked why and all of a sudden she can't tell me enough. Most obvious reason being that she ran into Paige Norbois in a hideaway restaurant with a guy who wasn't her husband. The two of them were in a corner holding hands and kissing. She wasn't sure Paige even knew she was there. But the next thing she knew, Nicole's piano lessons were canceled."

"Interesting. Did the guy sound like Faber?"

"Right on the button. Tall, thin, blond guy, dapper dresser."

"You getting any help from Chief Watkins on all of this?"

Ian's tone alters slightly. "Nobody's available, either for surveillance or interviews. By the way, I checked on the two kids: Derek Norbois is clean. Brother Stephen had an OUIL back in January. That's it."

Operating Under the Influence of Liquor. That might explain why there were only three cars at the site in a house with four drivers.

"Okay, I'm on my way. I'm still in Grand Rapids."

"Stan's with me in the car now," says Ian. "He says Ann Arbor needs traffic control. Says they got a town full of professors, but they can't seem to get the intervals right on the stoplights."

"Did he say he wouldn't send his kids to U of M on a bet?"

"Yeah, how did you know?"

Hugh laughs. "Just a guess. I'll meet you guys at the Best Western at one-thirty. Call Frisch and tell him we need to talk this afternoon."

———

"I think three of us is overkill on this visit," Hugh tells Stan West when he arrives. "Stan, you check out Nicole's friend, Lizzy Trout, while Ian and I break the bad news to Mr. Frisch. Then meet us at the station house."

He and Ian enter the offices of Challenge Press, and Anne Ransome escorts them to Roger Frisch's office. Frisch's suit and tie are impeccable as ever, but his face is pale, and his eyes look sunken. The air-conditioning is going full blast, and a ruffle of frigid air hits Hugh's face as he crosses the threshold.

"I've been sick as a dog for two days. Some kind of summer bug. I'm *never* sick." Frisch says this last statement distractedly, as if appealing to the judgment of someone not present in the room.

He clears his throat. "I can't think why it was necessary for you to call in a second accounting firm. We had an audit back in early April. Everything checked out fine. Seems redundant. A waste of money, in my opinion."

"What we got from the forensic accountants is

different from that report," Hugh says. "They found, first of all, that the payroll taxes are definitely in arrears. Also, there's this." He hands Frisch a sheet summarizing the list of forged checks.

Frisch studies it silently, then looks up. "Are they absolutely sure about this?"

"They are. They called in a handwriting expert."

Frisch's hands lightly tap the edges of the paper. "Who would do this? I can't imagine. But I suppose . . ." He looks up. "It could be anyone, couldn't it?"

Hugh nods. "Anyone with access to the company checks." Ian, standing next to the window, is staring out at the street.

"Well, that's just Anne Ransome and myself. Plus a couple of others in the acquisitions department who were working with me on the proposed purchase." Again, he clears his throat. "I need to clarify something here. Edward and myself—we are very different types, with different managing styles . . . but we understood each other. He was the entrepreneur—long on ideas, short on bureaucratic skills. He wasn't interested in the day-to-day running of the company. That's why he hired me. He was looking to expand further into publishing, maybe do as many as fifty or seventy-five titles a year. He was researching the alternative press market in other states. The company was doing well, in spite of a down market, and we knew we could afford to pick up one or two of these presses that were in trouble. I was working on the problem of capital. And I saw that if we held off paying the payroll taxes for only a few months, we could easily make the investment. Within a very short time we'd be in even better shape and could pay off the taxes, including the penalties."

"And this was done with his knowledge and permission?" Hugh asks.

"Not exactly. In this business, the right hand doesn't always want to know what the left is doing; that way the right can be completely straightforward about it, in case any questions come up."

"You knew what you were doing was illegal."

"According to government regulations, yes. But it takes months, sometimes years, for the government to follow up. That's the way it operates. And sometimes they change the rules midstream. As a matter of fact, we have yet to hear from the IRS about this. Only the state has shown any concern."

"So Mrs. Ransome becoming suspicious and blowing the whistle was what fouled things up."

A wry smile. "You might say so. Edward could have figured out what was going on if he'd wanted to. Or I would have told him. But he didn't want to know. Of course when Anne told him he insisted we put a hold on the purchases. That bothered me. I thought we should go ahead with it."

"And that was what the argument over the phone was about. Rather than a difference of opinion over collections?" Hugh asks.

"Yes. I should have told you the truth that day. I was taken by surprise. The auditors didn't discover it, and I didn't see why anyone else should. And it has nothing to do with this . . . this awful thing that's happened. It was a business decision. And it was on my head, not Edward's. He could always deny any knowledge in it. That was the whole point."

"But when he found out he was angry."

"At first, yes. But then we had a second talk."

"And when was that?"

"It was later that same day. He called me at the convention. Down at Cobo Hall. He'd calmed down quite a bit, told me he'd give me until he got back from vacation to work it all out."

"Why couldn't you just take the money you'd saved by not purchasing the other companies?"

"It wasn't that simple," Frisch says. "Some of that money had been used up in the negotiations. It would take a while to maneuver things into place. But I knew I'd be able to pull it off. He was giving me breathing space. I took it and was grateful for it." He smiles faintly. "Edward and I are much alike in certain ways; we're both family men. I knew he wasn't out to ruin me." And abruptly his manner turns brisk. "These things happen in business. The bottom line is, you do what's best for the company. In order to keep the company's credit and reputation intact. We both wanted the same thing. We were not on opposite sides in this."

"And after that second phone call—"

"After the second call I felt a lot better. I stayed around and talked to some people I knew at the convention. I was there for the rest of the day."

"You had dinner there?"

Frisch laughs. "I wouldn't call it dinner, exactly. I grabbed a doughnut and some coffee. I was supposed to pick up my wife and kids at the airport that night, but she called to say their flight was delayed. So I hung around until things started to wind down and then I drove back to Ann Arbor. I got home about seven-thirty. My family took a cab from Metro and got in around nine."

"I'll need a list of the people you talked to at the convention that day."

"It'll just take me a minute." Frisch grabs up a pen from his desk, reaches for some scrap paper.

"Also, we're going to run some DNA tests," Hugh says. "It'd be helpful if you'd give us a sample."

"So I'm the chief suspect." Frisch's voice is steady, but his hand trembles slightly as he writes.

"I'd say we're exploring every possibility at this point," Hugh says. "We're taking up a number of samples. The tests are the best way to rule you out if they come back negative."

"I'll need to talk with my lawyer first."

Hugh nods his head.

Outside in the street, Ian asks: "Well? What d'you think?"

"I think he gave it up pretty fast about the payroll taxes. Considering a few days ago it was just some crazy notion Anne Ransome dreamed up."

"Yeah. He saw the handwriting on the wall, with the forged checks. Makes you think the same thing's going to happen with them, too."

"Hard to say. There are a few people who could have had access to those checks."

"Doesn't make him seem too reliable," Ian says.

"Here's the thing," Hugh says. "There's no way he could have driven up to Blessed and back in time to be home when his wife and kids arrived. That's a solid nine hours of driving, nine and a half, ten with traffic."

"So, if he left by ten in the morning, he could be back by seven or seven-thirty."

"Barely. With no time factored in for the murders."

"He wouldn't need much. Fifteen minutes max. Clean up, pick up the shells, slap a piece of cardboard over the window, close the drapes, and he's outta there."

Hugh frowns. "Maybe."

"What if he hired someone else to do it?" Ian asks.

"He would've had to plan it in advance," says Hugh. "And it didn't seem like things were at the level of crisis before that phone call the morning of the murders."

"Yeah, that's true. But those conventioneers better come through for him," says Ian. "Otherwise he's up shit creek without a frickin' alibi."

"We'd better keep an eye on him," Hugh says. "Post a watch at his house tonight."

Ian sighs. "Yeah, I was afraid you were going to say that."

REASONABLE DOUBT

HUGH ARRIVES AT the offices of James Faber and is ushered in by the broker himself. The heat of the day is ruthless; the sweat running down Hugh's back feels cold in the air-conditioned building.

"The last time I saw Paige was the Sunday before they left for Blessed," Faber says. "We met at the arboretum and took a walk. That was when she told me she was breaking it off with me." He shrugs. "But I didn't believe it. I've been through this with her before. Her schedule always runs the show. In the summer she spends a lot more time with her family. It's harder for her to get away. I thought I'd just give her room to think things over. I was going to call her when they got back from Banff."

"You weren't prepared to just let it go."

"No. And she knew I wouldn't." He turns away from Hugh, toward the window. "Every so often it just got too painful for her. She'd have to rededicate herself. To being the perfect wife, you know, the perfect mother."

"So your relationship pretty much ran on her terms."

"Oh, yeah. And it always took a backseat to her kids."

"How did the two of you meet?"

He smiles. "I'm sure Elaine Spiteri told you. She and Paige were friends. It was through Elaine. I'd heard a lot about Paige before I ever met her. It started out more or less as a business relationship. She had some money, she wanted to invest it. So she came to see me and we had a few meetings. I helped her set up the trust for her kids."

"You knew them?"

"Mostly I knew *about* them. She and I would talk whenever we were together—about Stephen's relationship with Edward, or Nicole's trouble in school, David's moodiness—things that she couldn't discuss with Edward. He always shot from the hip. She never felt she could be completely honest with him, he was too unpredictable."

"So she kept a lot of secrets."

Faber looks at Hugh. "The way wives do, yeah. We'd talk things over first and try to figure out a strategy."

"Do you think Edward Norbois knew his wife was unhappy?"

Faber smiles. "Who says she was unhappy? As for Edward, it'd be hard to know what he knew about anything. He played his cards pretty close up."

"Did he know about the affair?"

"Oh, Jesus, no. I'm sure not. Edward's vision was pretty narrow. As long as Paige was around to cook the meals and satisfy his every need, he was fine with it."

"Did she ever talk about divorcing him?"

Faber hesitates. "Not really. I think she just wanted relief. From the rigidity, you know . . . it was exhausting."

"Who else knew about the two of you?"

"You mean, besides Elaine? Not many. My ex-wife. She and I have stayed friends and we'd occasionally talk things over. My sister knows about it. I'd say that's it. Why?"

"Just trying to see where it falls—between top secret and common knowledge."

"It wasn't common knowledge." The tone is slightly stiff, but he quickly smooths it out. "Not that Edward would've thrown her out, or anything close. He was dependent on her. In spite of the way he treated her—almost like she was a kid herself. That was the problem—she knew she was indispensable. How could she ever think of leaving him?"

"And that didn't bother you?"

"I wanted her to stop feeling guilty about us. To make peace with it. I tried to get her to see how her image of being perfect was pointless."

"And what about you? Were you satisfied with the relationship?"

Faber thinks about it. "For now it was enough. We probably could have gone on with things pretty much the way they were. Look, I loved her," he says. "She loved me. We trusted each other. We were together almost three years. She had somebody she could talk to, somebody who was on her side. And I got plenty in return." He glances briefly out the window, then down at the calendar on his desk. He seems suddenly uncomfortable with the way the conversation is going. When he looks up, it is to fix his glance squarely on Hugh's face. "I had a son. He died of leukemia when he was ten. It ended my marriage. Also any thoughts I had of living the conventional life."

"I'm sorry," Hugh says, meaning it.

Faber clasps his hands, looking down at them curiously. "It was five years ago," he says. "But it changed my life. I don't have a lot of long-term expectations. And I'm never too surprised when things don't turn out the way I planned."

"I understand," Hugh says.

"Listen," Faber says, "I want to see this thing solved. Whatever I can do to help, I'll be happy to do it. I want you to get the bastard who did this."

"It would help if you'd be willing to give us a DNA sample," Hugh says.

"Why?"

"We're trying to screen people out. Get them off the list."

"Are you saying . . . was there a rape? I thought . . . I didn't know. The papers didn't say anything . . . how were they able to determine that?" Faber abruptly sits on the edge of the desk, staring into space. "This is awful," he says, passing a hand over his eyes. "It makes me sick."

"I'm sorry," Hugh says. His mind spins back to the scene when he and Ian first arrived. It *was* awful. And how quickly one becomes used to the idea of it. Life goes on and there is work to be done. It's the one aspect of this job that he absolutely hates.

He leaves Faber's office and goes to visit Derek's old roommate. He'd gotten the name from a note on the bulletin board in the kitchen in Blessed. *Derek: call Phil Stanberg when you get a chance 313-555-7756.*

The apartment on Forest Avenue is neat, as is Phil himself—T-shirt freshly pressed, dark hair cut close to his head. He looks genuinely anguished.

"I can't believe this," he says. "I talked to Derek in June. We were going kayaking when he got back from Banff—"

"How long had you known him?"

"About two years. We met when we roomed together as freshmen. I knew his whole family. They were great people, especially his mom. His dad was, you know, a good guy, but standoffish. Like someone who had to be sure of the facts before he'd decide if you were okay for his son to hang around with."

"Did he have any girlfriends?"

"Not many. There was one girl he knew back in high school who used to call him up. Dianne Cain. She went to Ypsi. I think she thought he was her boyfriend, but it was all in her head." Phil smiles at this.

"Can you give me the names of some of the guys he hung out with?"

"Sure." He goes to the counter for paper and

pencil. "His friends were a little weird, I gotta say. You know, arty guys. Musicians. Derek loved classical music. Mahler and Beethoven. He was definitely different from your average college guy. A lot of his friends were potheads, too. But Derek didn't smoke. He just wasn't interested. His brother did, though. Steve used to stop by the apartment with his high school buddies."

"How come you and Derek didn't room together this year?"

"My girlfriend moved in with me. She graduated from high school a year ago. We always planned to get an apartment together. So Derek took a place over on East U. He roomed with somebody he'd met over at the Union. I didn't see much of him this past year, but I talked to him a lot on the phone. One thing about Derek," Phil says. "He was smart. Around this place people are always pushing their big brains at you—'Sorry, didn't see you there, Little Head . . .' Derek wasn't like that. He never showed off, but he was one of the brainier guys I knew." He points to several framed pictures on the wall. "That's some of his artwork."

"I thought I recognized it."

Hugh examines the sketches. The same characteristic lines, woven through with subtle shadow; the same crisp, bold finishing strokes.

"That's Therese. My girlfriend. He did it for her last year."

Hugh hands him his card. "Thanks for your help."

"Anytime," Phil says.

CRUEL AND UNUSUAL

Hugh arrives at the large brick colonial in Ann Arbor Hills and checks the address once again: *Mitchell Cain, P.A.* As soon as he pulls up in front, a young woman waves to him from the front door. "I'll be right out!"

Funny how some people can't stand the notion of cops inside their houses. It's as if they are the carriers of a strange disease that can't be banished, once it has crossed the threshold. Hugh has observed over the years that cop avoidance seems to work in direct correlation to people's involvement in a crime: the farther you are from it, the more you want to stay away.

Dianne Cain hurries across the lawn to the curb. She is smoothly pretty, wearing a gray slip of a dress and metallic gray flats. Her blond hair is shaved up one side of her head in a quarter-inch crew cut. *Why do they do this?* Hugh wonders. With Becky turning eleven this September he fears he won't have long to wait to find this out.

"I haven't seen Derek since last March," Dianne says, getting into the patrol car. "I was surprised you even had my name. How'd you get it?"

"Derek's roommate. He told me you two went to high school together."

Dianne makes a face. "I don't much care for that one. He's a user. Thinks he's God's gift to women."

"You're talking about Phil Stanberg?"

"Oh no. Not Phil. I thought you meant this year's roommate. Over on East University. Guy Mason."

Hugh takes out his pen and notebook, jots down the name and address. "Can you tell me something about Derek? What kind of guy he was?"

She thinks a minute. "He was the sweetest boy I ever knew. A really good person. But as nice as he was, he was . . . basically a loner. You couldn't get close to him. When I saw him this spring he had something on his mind, I just knew it. But he wouldn't tell me. I think I finally just gave up on him." She frowns. "Now I'm feeling guilty. I wish we'd stayed in closer touch."

"You and he were just friends?" Hugh asks.

"Just friends," she agrees. A small silence: Then she smiles. "Well. I had aspirations at one time. Lots of girls did. But you could wait forever for Derek to get a clue. Once I even asked him if he was gay. He just laughed and said he didn't think so."

"That sweetness trait," Hugh says. "It's one people can take advantage of."

Dianne nods. "Derek's parents had a lot of money. He was very generous with it. A lot more than I thought he should be. It's another reason I didn't like Guy very much. I saw him say stuff like, 'Pick me up a six-pack while you're out, will you?' And I never saw him pay Derek back. It was the same in high school. Derek was always an easy target."

"Did Derek ever do any sketches of you?" Hugh asks.

She nods. "Back when we were in high school. He gave one of them to me for my birthday. But what was I supposed to do with a picture of myself? Hang it up on my wall? I think I stuck it away in a drawer somewhere."

Milo Brent, another of Phil Stanberg's contacts, is obviously one of the designated weirdos. His straight, stringy hair and thick glasses mark him out; that, and the lopsided goofy grin. Hugh finds him at his job, clerking in an office at the university's Administration Building.

"This is unreal," Milo says. "Some kind of freak accident. It's not supposed to happen to people you know."

No accident, Hugh thinks. Someone highly organized, capable of executing a carefully thought-out plan.

"Derek's a guy with no enemies," Milo says. "I mean *none.* But then, you gotta think—who has enemies like this? It has to be some Andrew Cunanan type, don't you think? His brother Steve hung out with some yahoos, but nobody this crazy."

"You know any of these yahoos by name?"

Milo shakes his head. "They were all just high school kids. They tagged along at a few of our beer parties. You know what's really strange about this whole thing to me? Derek was such a Do-Right. I remember once a bunch of us sneaked into a movie. Only Derek wouldn't—he actually got in line and paid for his ticket. He said if he didn't he'd never be able to run for president. I mean, he was laughing at the time, but I think he really meant it. He couldn't bring himself to cheat on anything, not even a lousy movie ticket."

———

"I'd like to help," Dan Fellowes tells Hugh. "I wish I knew something. But I haven't seen Derek since he left school early in June. I ran into him on the street and he said he was going up to their cabin for the summer. He seemed kind of bummed the day I saw him. I thought it was because he was leaving Ann Arbor, and I told him it didn't sound all that bad—sailing, loafing around on the beach while your dad forks out the dough."

———

Hugh parks the patrol car in front of a small deli—Jimmy's Pizza and Subs. Delivery available for everything every day 555-1313—on a quiet, tree-shaded street near campus. The mustard-yellow house directly across the way looks lumpy and disheveled. Most of the houses on this street could use at minimum a coat of paint. It's a neighborhood of typical student housing: the main campus of the university is a five-minute walk away, Bus Ad school just around the corner.

Inside the yellow house, the hallway is plastered

with various warnings and reprimands: *Another Dopeless Hope Fiend—Orgazmo—making sex safe again—Don't laugh, mister, your daughter might be in here.*

God forbid. He rings the bell labeled Mason/Norbois. A moment later, a dark-haired girl wearing black shorts and a black halter top leans over the wooden balcony above him.

"What d'you want?"

He looks up at her. "Hugh DeWitt. Emmet County Sheriff's Department. I'm looking for Guy Mason."

She clatters down the stairs until she's standing just slightly above him, her ankles on a level with his eyes. Her legs are trim and tanned. She looks to be about twenty, wearing black, strappy sandals on her feet, a gold ring in her navel.

"Emmet County," she says. "You're here about Derek, then."

"Right. You a student here?"

She laughs. "Not hardly. I own the building."

His first thought is that she doesn't seem old enough—or responsible enough—to own much of anything. *And what are you basing this on?* It better not be the navel ring; Karen would nail him for that.

"I'm Maura," she says, extending her hand to him; it is small, surprisingly delicate. "Maura James."

"Good to meet you," Hugh says.

"Guy's at work right now," she says. "He should be home soon."

"Where does he work?"

"A bike shop downtown. Butch's. Can you say what's been going on with the investigation? The papers are pretty vague."

"We're still in the preliminary stages."

"Yeah." She brushes this aside. "But what do you really think? You must have an idea."

"Do you have some time?" he asks. "I'd like to talk to you."

"Sure. About Derek, you mean? I haven't seen him since the middle of May, when he moved back to his parents' house. He said he couldn't afford the rent anymore." She makes a face. "Hard to believe that one. I just said, 'Whatever.'"

"How did you get along with Derek?" Hugh asks. "Was he a good tenant?"

She shrugs. "He didn't owe me money; that's all I cared about." Then, almost as an afterthought: "He was a nice guy. Sort of dweeby, but cute. He wasn't . . . he didn't have a lot of *awareness,* y'know? Like he was shy. Not like his roommate." She laughs. "But don't tell *him* I said so." She takes a quick glance around the hallway, littered with newspapers and fast-food trash. "Somebody needs to do some serious cleaning up around here."

"How long have you owned this place?"

"Couple of years. My uncle found it for me. He thought it'd be a good investment. He said it would keep me off the streets."

"Is your uncle a realtor?"

"No. He's just . . . he takes care of my finances. Listen, do you want to come upstairs? I mean, we might as well sit down if we're going to talk."

He follows her up the stairs to her apartment, which takes up the entire third floor. It is nearly bare of furniture. Between the narrow front windows is a futon covered in purple paisley. A card table and two chairs sit on the adjacent wall. A small refrigerator, stove, and sink. On the wall opposite the bed, a handsome oak armoire. Maura sees him eyeing it.

"It's an antique," she says. "My uncle had it in his house in Dexter. This used to be the attic, so it doesn't have any closets. You want a beer?" She moves to the refrigerator, opens it, and offers him a can.

He smiles, shaking his head. She pops the lid. Perching on the edge of the countertop, she indicates the card table chair: "Sit down, why don't you?"

He sits. "So Derek didn't owe you any money."

"Nope. He always paid his rent on time. By mail." She grins. "I think it was so he wouldn't have to talk to me. Like I told you, he was shy."

"How many tenants do you have?" Hugh asks.

"Right now I'm down, because of summer break. Usually there's ten—a triple and two singles on the first floor, a triple and a double on the second."

"How do people find this place?"

"It's a good location. Word gets around."

"You know your tenants fairly well?"

"I don't keep track of their comings and goings, if that's what you mean." She looks at him shrewdly. "What's with all the questions about my tenants? You aren't thinking somebody in this building killed those people, are you? That's nuts."

"I'm just talking to anyone who knew members of the family. Would you mind giving me a list of your tenants' names?"

"Help yourself." She reaches into a drawer underneath the counter and takes out a large notebook. She hands it to him.

He looks through the ledger, surprised to see how meticulously it is kept: the names listed in the front, with home addresses and telephone numbers, followed by individual pages of monthly Accounts Receivable. There are a number of miscellaneous notations: *"1A: will pay 2/11 when check from Mom arrives"; "faucet leaks in bathroom on two, call Eddie"; "2B: reminded about garbage left in hall 3/23"; "1C: no loud music after midnight! Second reminder 11/5."*

He copies names and phone numbers into his notebook while Maura watches, cradling the beer between her knees.

"Your tenants ever give you any trouble? You know—wild parties, other disturbances?"

She shakes her head. "This group I have now is pretty tame. I make it clear up-front that's how I like it."

"Did Derek ever bring women back to the place?"

An impatient sigh. "Look, my roomers don't mind my business. I do them the same favor. I'm pretty sure none of them are homicidal maniacs. I haven't had any DVs since I owned the building."

DV. Domestic Violence. She's up on the lingo; he wonders if she got it from TV or something more personal.

"Just trying to get the lay of the land," he says, smiling at her and glancing at his wristwatch. *After one o'clock.* Derek's roommate should be home by now. "Anyway, thanks for your time."

The door to Guy Mason's apartment is open; Hugh knocks on the frame. The living room has a scuffed leather couch and matching chair, plus one other, made of white wicker. A red-enameled table sits in a corner with a mammoth TV on top of it. The floor is of bare wood.

A young man with a thin, athletic body and light curly hair comes out of the kitchen. "Looking for me?" he asks pleasantly.

"Are you Guy Mason?"

"Yeah. C'mon in. You're from the sheriff's office, right? I saw your car out front."

The apartment is neatly kept, like Guy himself; his T-shirt is clean; his khakis look freshly pressed.

"This is such a damned shock," he says. "Everybody's blown away by it. I knew the whole family. I was supposed to go up to their place in Blessed when they got back from Banff."

"Can you tell me something about them?" Hugh asks. "What they were like?"

"They were great people. I keep trying to figure this thing out. It had to be some nutcase, don't you think? I mean up there, where everything's so goddamned peaceful and beautiful. How could this happen?"

"That's what we're trying to figure out," Hugh says. "Derek was an artist, right?" He indicates the sketches mounted on the wall above the couch. "Is that some of his work?"

Guy nods. "He did those while he was sitting on the Diag. Just before school got out. I swear he could whip one off in five minutes or less. He had a photographic memory. He'd keep working even after the people walked away. This one's my favorite." He points to the sketch of a long-legged girl lying on the lawn, her profile half-hidden behind a fall of dark hair. She's wearing a short skirt and bulky crew sweater, the sleeves rolled above her elbows, hands holding a half-eaten apple.

"He was planning to transfer into art school this fall," Guy says. "He talked about it all the time. I told him he should've been there right from the beginning."

"Can you tell me something about his family life? How did he get along with his dad?"

"Pretty well, I guess. That guy was all business, though. Very intense. Last February I went up to their cabin cross-country skiing for the weekend. Mr. Norbois talked to me about getting back in school. *'You've got potential, Guy. You can't work in a bike shop all your life.'* I thought it was nice of him to take an interest." He shrugs. "I guess maybe it'd be different, though, if he was my dad. I know Derek felt a lot of pressure."

"You're not a student?" Hugh asks.

"I was until I ran out of money. You need dough to go here. But Ann Arbor's great." He grins. "Lots of good-looking women. So I thought I'd stick around till I can figure out what to do with my life."

"Did Derek have many girlfriends?" Hugh asks.

"You mean, besides our landlady? Not that I know of."

"Derek and Maura had a thing going?"

"Yeah, for a while. Right after he moved in. Didn't she tell you? Maybe she didn't think it was police business. Geez. Me and my big mouth. Anyway, it didn't last long." Guy looks around the living room. "This place looked a lot better when he lived here. We had some decent furniture. But he moved back home. He knew the shit would hit the fan as soon as his dad found out he was planning to transfer out of Bus Ad school. God, it's so fucking weird to think they're gone. That *he's* gone. I don't believe it. I guess I just don't want to believe it."

Hugh hands the boy his card and Guy studies it. "DeWitt," he says. "Good cop name. I once knew a cop named Officer Blood—d'you believe that? Lived right down the street from me. You ever listen to that Randy Newman song 'Jolly Coppers on Parade'? Good song, sad but good. I've even thought about being a cop myself."

"Is that right?"

"Yeah. The closest I came was taking a course called Psychology of the Deviant Individual. That was an eye-opener." He looks up at Hugh. "How long d'you think it'd take me?"

"To become a cop? A couple of years."

"But you got to be smart, right?"

"Not so smart. Just smarter than the guys you're trying to catch."

"You make decent money at it?"

Hugh grins. "Not really. But look at the rewards. All that prestige."

They both laugh.

"Give me a call if you think of anything else, will you?" Hugh asks.

"I'll do that," Guy promises.

CATCHING UP

"WHEN WILL YOU be home?" Karen asks when
he calls her from the motel. "I'm missing you."

"I don't know. Soon. Maybe tomorrow. You
feeling nervous? Why don't you go to your
mother's?"

"I'm not nervous," she says. "I'm missing you."

"What's happening up there? Fredda says
there's all kinds of strangers in town."

"Yes. It's hard to get to the grocery store without running into them. There were two reporters
in front of the house tonight. Just a sec . . ." She

leaves the phone, returns in a moment. "Nobody out there now, thank heavens."

"Tell 'em to move on, tell 'em to call me at work. Jesus, the next thing you know, there'll be people driving up from the city to get their pictures taken at the murder site. It'll be just like L.A."

"Hugh, there is absolutely nothing you can do about it." Her tone is firm. "So don't worry about it. We're doing fine."

"Becky should be having a nice, peaceful summer. Instead there's anthills of media people . . ."

"You never listen," she says. "Your daughter's having a fine summer. She's swimming every day. Looking forward to leaving for horse camp."

"I suppose I should start worrying about her getting flipped off a damn stallion and breaking a leg."

"By all means," Karen says, "if it makes you feel any better."

"Thanks. You're a comfort." He sighs. "It's too hot here."

"Here, too."

"Stay inside," he advises. "Out of the sun."

"I'll try. Gotta go now," she says. "Love you."

He echoes it, hanging up the phone. She is absolutely right, there's nothing he can do about nine tenths of the stuff he worries about. He knows exactly why he does it: Stay on top of things and you can prevent the worst from happening. He still believes this, even though he's been proved wrong dozens of times.

———

"We found all six of the guys Frisch says he talked to at the convention," Ian tells him over dinner. "None of them remembers seeing him on the twenty-fifth."

"None?"

"Nope. One guy thinks he may have passed him in the hall. But he was only there in the morning, so they wouldn't have overlapped for more than an hour." Ian passes Hugh the list across the table. "The second guy's kid had a bike accident that day, so he spent most of it at the hospital. Didn't get to Cobo Hall until after three. Can't swear to seeing Frisch but thinks he might have. The other four say absolutely not."

"Some alibi," Stan West says.

"Did you have a chance to talk to Lizzy Trout?" Hugh asks him.

"Yeah. Bright little girl. She was up at the cabin with the Norbois family over Memorial Day weekend. Don't think that isn't freaking her parents out. She says one of the older boys had a buddy up that same time, she doesn't know if it was Stephen's or Derek's friend. Says the three of them went out Saturday night and didn't come home until four in the morning. Norbois read 'em the riot act at breakfast."

"Where in hell were they in Blessed until four o'clock in the morning?"

"You got me." Stan grins at him. "The mother told me that Steve Norbois and his dad were like oil and water. Her opinion is that Norbois held the reins pretty tight. Evidently she and Paige talked about this many times. Derek Norbois was the perfect kid—honor student, et cetera. The type who'd be a tough act to follow."

"I've been thinking," Ian says suddenly. "What if it wasn't premeditated? What if Frisch drove up there intending to talk things over, but once he arrived he realized Norbois wasn't going for it? You know—his plan to straighten things out? Or maybe Frisch couldn't get his hands on the money like he promised—"

"He *happened* to drive up there with a .32 semiautomatic in his glove compartment?" Stan says. "Yeah, that makes sense."

"None of it makes sense," Hugh says. "Least of all the fact that he got caught in a lie about the missing money. He's doing such a crappy job of covering things up, he doesn't seem half smart enough for this job. Now he tells us there was a second phone call, where all was forgiven. I'm not buying it."

"Yeah," Ian says. "That did seem a little too

convenient. I only remember seeing the one call on the phone records, but I guess Norbois could've made it from a cell phone. So, are you liking this guy for the murders?"

"Enough to keep an eye on him. You and Stan take the first watch tonight. I'll take over at midnight." He can tell by their exchange of looks they were hoping to head home tonight. "Kevin says he'll have a duty roster ready for us tomorrow. He promised."

"No shit," says Stan. "You mean they're actually gonna help us?"

Tonight the *Ann Arbor News* has a long article about the crime in Blessed: *Accountants discover forged checks . . . Comptroller is chief suspect in multiple murders . . . Sheriff's office near making an arrest.* Hugh tosses the paper onto the bed. Obviously someone took it upon himself to create some news. He hopes it wasn't anybody from his crew.

He takes his shoes off, lies down on his back, hands behind his head. He doesn't envy Kevin, living with the tension of one coed murder after another for an entire year, and, on top of it, having to deal with media bullshit on a daily basis.

Four young women in the prime of life. Four

families destroyed by grief. Now, another entire family wiped out in one night of butchery. Where does evil like this originate? What is its meaning in the world? It's a blessing there were no survivors. How could anyone who lived through that carnage ever hope to become sane again?

Lying here he feels chilled, depressed. Something is nagging at him, trying to surface; he can feel it down in his gut. *Face it, DeWitt: Is this the life you want for yourself? Following around behind these envoys of evil, trying to fathom them? Cleaning up their messes?*

What triggers these kinds of thoughts? Somehow it seems to be all mixed up with that little girl: Nicole Norbois. With Becky, too. He can't keep them separate in his mind anymore. Can't stop the feeling of foreboding around the one who's still alive. Can't allow the dead one's spirit to rest in peace.

NICOLE

I DON'T LIKE HIM. Neither does Lizzy; she told me that before, when he came up over the weekend. Something about his eyes and the way he smiles. Not at me, he never smiles at me, only at Mom. I want to tell her what a creep he is but she probably wouldn't listen. Nobody ever listens to me, they're all too busy to pay attention to what I'm saying. All except Dad. I know he wouldn't like it either if he knew.

I remember Mrs. Messenger asking me if it was my uncle driving the tan Mercedes, and when

I told Mom she said, *That's the end of piano lessons with that nosey parker,* which was fine with me, I didn't like Mrs. Messenger anyway. But Mom likes *him.* And if she knew how nosy *he* was, it might make a difference. He's always sniffing around, asking about personal stuff. He's got the creepiest laugh. Everything about him is creepy. What's he doing up here anyway? I know he wasn't invited, because we're going away. He'll probably want to come in and play cards with us now, acting like he's part of the family, trying to be friendly. But I know better.

I've made up my mind about what I'm going to be when I grow up. A girl detective like Nancy Drew. Derek says I even look like her, with my blond hair and blue eyes. He drew a picture of me once, in that blue suit Nancy always wears. Driving a blue roadster. Derek says a roadster is just a fancy name for a convertible. That drawing disappeared. I know it was in my desk up here, but now I can't find it anymore. I bet *he* took it. *Mr. Nosy.*

Or else it was Davey. He can't keep his hands off my stuff either. Although why he'd want it I can't imagine. I know Davey took five dollars from my elephant bank, because I saw him coming out of my room. He acts like I dreamed it. *I was never in your room. Come back to the real world, Nikki.* He is such a liar. Does he think I can't count? Lizzy thinks he's cute, but she wouldn't think so if it was *her* brother doing this stuff. I left him a note in his room: *I know it was you and you better put it back or I am telling Dad tonight!!!!* And the next morning, there it was on my dresser. Davey would rather live in a cave with no food and water for the rest of his life than to have Dad mad at him.

I don't want anyone to get mad over this thing that happened—least of all Dad—but I think I should tell it. I should have told somebody back when it first happened. Because now won't it look strange that I never said anything before? I was the only one who saw him messing with stuff that wasn't his, being a nosey parker like Mrs. Messenger. It was the look on his face that gave it away more than anything. If I hadn't come up to the house to change my bathing suit nobody would have known. He told me to forget about it. *What does it look like I'm doing?* With that creepy smile on his face. I get tired of this family always telling me how I have too big of an imagination. What does that even mean?

And now here he is again, hanging around just when we're getting ready to leave, standing out there in the bushes like that. Why doesn't he knock on the door like a normal person? What's that thing in his hand? I can't see what he's doing,

it's getting so dark out there and his face is all
weird. Maybe he's spying on us. Maybe he's not
even real it's only the bushes moving in the wind.
But there's no wind no wind not tonight not now
no no no no no

WHO KNOWS WHAT

A<small>LL'S</small> <small>WELL</small> <small>IN</small> Claremont Green," Stan says as Hugh pulls alongside their vehicle.

"You want us back here in the morning?" Ian asks.

"No. Ann Arbor's taking over. You guys can head on home whenever you want."

"When will you be back there?"

"Late tomorrow, I hope. I'm going to try to get both Frisch and Faber over to the lab in the morning and then drop the samples off at Blodgett on my way."

He takes their spot on the street and settles back against the seat. The light in the living room of the Frisch house, behind him, casts a soft glow into the front yard. He keeps his eyes on the rearview mirror. He's not sleepy, has no need for pills or the like; he has never had a problem staying awake on surveillance. This is what he thought of as a cop's life, back in high school. *Romance*. He smiles to himself, remembering how his dad tried to warn him.

He lowers the windows, aware at once of a pungent, vaguely familiar odor. A particular flower. Karen has told him what it is, but he can't remember. He combs his brain for the name as the front door of the Frisch house opens and a figure stands in the doorway. He sits bolt upright as someone descends the front steps, heading for the garage door. *It has to be Frisch*. But where is he going?

A second later the garage door opens, and the figure disappears inside. Hugh reaches for the ignition key. When he sees the taillights, he'll be ready to move. His heart thrums inside his chest. The figure emerges from the darkness of the garage, trundling a large tub. It clunks along on its bulky wheels, stopping just at the edge of the curb. Now he notices, up and down the street, all of the other garbage cans. *Of course. Tomorrow is pickup day.*

The figure is moving steadily up the sidewalk toward the car. Hugh switches off the engine.

"You worried about me?" Roger Frisch asks, bending to peer inside. "I'm not going anywhere."

"Just routine," Hugh assures him.

"Why not come inside? Have a drink? As long as you're waiting." He straightens up. "It's cooler in there."

Hugh laughs. "You know, I wouldn't mind."

Together they walk back to the house. He can tell Frisch has been drinking; the smell of liquor is in the air between them.

"This is my life," Frisch says. "I take out the garbage. I drop off the dry cleaning and get the car washed on my way to work. Pretty dull stuff."

"Sounds like my life," Hugh says.

"I read in the paper today," says Frisch, "that you may be close to making an arrest in the case."

"I don't read the papers," Hugh says drily.

"Just tell me what you think," Frisch says, as though they are talking about the latest stock prices. "I mean, why would the company put up a one-hundred-thousand-dollar reward if I knew who the killer was? Doesn't that seem like pushing it?"

"Good question."

They enter, and Hugh is surprised by the feel of genuine comfort: buttery-soft leather chairs, landscape paintings, bookshelves with leaded glass doors awash in creamy lamplight. Somehow he didn't expect to be charmed by this house.

A half-empty glass sits on the coffee table. Frisch drains it quickly, and the ice clicks against his teeth.

"What's your pleasure? I've got scotch, bourbon—"

"Nothing for me, thanks."

"Some ice water?"

"Sure."

He fills a glass from the pitcher on the table and hands it to Hugh. Then he pours a shot of scotch for himself, takes a healthy swallow.

"You seem like a fair-minded man," he says. "If I told you I didn't do it, would you believe me? My lawyer says I'm nuts to give you the DNA sample. He says I don't have to do it unless you arrest me."

Hugh shrugs. "He's right."

"I say it makes me look guilty if I don't. But then, whatever I do, it makes me look guilty, doesn't it? That's the hell of it." He sits down on the couch, waving Hugh to the chair across from it. "I think I'm going to get nailed for this. I'm innocent, but I'm going to get nailed."

"The best way to prove your innocence," Hugh says, "is to do the test."

"Right." He takes another swallow. "There's something I've been meaning to tell you. I worked for a small press in Denver a few years ago. Mountaintop Editions. They went belly-up. Not my fault, but the guy sued me anyway."

"Yeah," Hugh says. "I heard about it."

"Thought you might have. Well, I didn't murder that guy, either. And I can tell you it was a worse fiasco than this." He sits back, swirling his glass in the light, looking through it meditatively. "Publishing is an incestuous trade. We all know each other's business. Edward knew about my problems with Mountaintop. He didn't care. It was what I was doing for *him* that mattered."

"Like forging checks?"

Silence.

"Did you forge them?" Hugh keeps his tone neutral, as if inquiring about the performance of some household task. *Did you take out the garbage?*

"Don't be in too much of a hurry to judge me on that one." Frisch stares at him calmly. "Yeah, I did it. I knew I could put the money back. Anytime I wanted to. Nobody would *ever* have known about it, don't you see? All this is coming out now *because* they were murdered. It isn't the reason they were murdered. Isn't it obvious? Someone killed them, someone randomly picked them out. And now, because of some combination of circumstances having nothing at all to do with these killings, it's all coming down on me." His hand on the glass tightens. "I was helping Edward to survive—to *thrive*—in a cutthroat world that doesn't stop screwing you long enough to apologize. I was bringing him customers, I was bringing him business!"

"And you were embezzling money."

"I was planning to put it all back. With interest."

"But you didn't get the chance."

"That's right. I didn't have enough time." He sets the glass down on the table. "My wife thinks I'm blowing this all out of proportion. She says I have a tendency to do that. The papers are wrong, she says."

"Listen," Hugh says, "I'm not out to nail anybody for this except the person who did it. And I'm willing to pay attention to extenuating circumstances. But I have to know what they are."

"All right, then. My wife's sister is very ill. She has cancer and she doesn't have any insurance. I've been taking money over the last year. From inactive accounts. To help her. There was no reason to think they'd ever be looked at . . ."

"How much money?" Hugh asks, fingering the notebook in his pocket. He'd like to take it out, but he doesn't want Frisch to get rattled. *Let him talk first.*

"Eighty thousand. Maybe a little more. It was a loan. To get us over the hump."

"And Anne Ransome finding out about the unpaid taxes turned the lights up on everything."

"Eighty thousand dollars," Frisch repeats. "You have no idea how little that meant to Edward. It was nothing. It was vacation money." He snaps his fingers. "One plane trip and it's gone. I had the deal all set with an Ypsilanti press that would have turned everything around. It would have been my bonus. It fell through at the last minute, because of Anne. But that doesn't mean I couldn't have gotten another one going." He slumps in the chair.

"Tell me about that second phone call," Hugh says. "The one you took at the convention."

Frisch looks up. "There was no second call," he says calmly. "But you already knew that, didn't you? I could tell by the look on your face." He sits up again, back on track. "But there *could have been.* Because I *knew* Edward. He would have given me another chance. I might've even kept my job. He was angry that day, but he would have gotten over it. Edward was nothing if not pragmatic. And I was damned good at my job. He knew it was in my best interest to put things right. The whole company didn't have to go down because of this. It wouldn't have." He raises his hands. "Now everything's a mess. The company could go under. Everybody loses." He takes another drink of his scotch. "I meant it about the reward money. I want to see this person caught. I'll take a lie detector test, too."

"That won't be necessary," Hugh says. "The DNA test is all I need right now."

"Tell me the truth. Are you going to arrest me?"

"I haven't spoken to a reporter since the day after the bodies were found," Hugh says, knowing this isn't an answer.

Studying the oriental rug in front of him—done in shades of opulent green like the leaves of the cedar trees—he avoids Frisch's eyes. "The lab offices are in police headquarters. It's a ten-minute procedure. I can pick you up and bring you back here."

A long silence. "All right. But I need to run a few errands first. I'll meet you there. How's ten o'clock?"

"Fine."

Frisch walks him to the door. "I don't know what to do next," he says. "Mainly about the employees. Some of them have asked if they should start looking for work. No way of knowing at this point. I guess you just keep moving forward."

"That's what I'd do," Hugh says. He has no idea what moving forward means. Or what it would look like to this man. Walking to his car, he looks at his watch: nearly two o'clock. He notices the evening has cooled down slightly. He slides beneath the steering wheel and opens both front windows to the soft, fetid air. *That was a weird scene.* He doesn't know exactly what to make of Roger Frisch and his sudden candor. *The relaxed truthfulness of tired liars.* One of his father's favorite expressions. Was that the whole truth? Hard to tell. Frisch has told so many lies already.

Hugh pours himself some iced tea from his thermos, watching the dance of shadows as they move across the lawn. He guesses that Frisch won't feel much like getting up in the morning; he was slurring his words pretty loosely toward the end. Again he can smell the exotic odor in the air. *Bee balm.* And it has another name, too: monarda. There. Not bad for a guy who never listens.

———

The Ann Arbor duty cops show up promptly at seven-thirty, for which Hugh is grateful. He'll have time for a shower and breakfast at the motel before he heads for the station house. He made the plan with James Faber to meet him at the lab at nine sharp.

"I've got appointments later on in the morning," Faber had said. Hugh saw that the import of the whole thing was beginning to register. But Faber didn't back down.

"It's a simple procedure. It'll only take a few

minutes," he had assured him. Just as he assured Frisch last night. A simple procedure that records a permanent, indisputable record of someone's complete genetic makeup.

When he lets himself into his room the red light on the phone is blinking.

"Hugh, we're out of here." It's Ian's voice on the machine. "Fredda called. There's somebody up near the Norbois place who supposedly heard something he thinks we ought to know about. I'll check it out when I get there."

Hugh strips and turns on the shower. He wonders when they left. The warm water feels comforting against his back. His muscles are tense, but he's not tired. Is this the first stakeout in history where the inspector was invited in for a drink by the inspectee?

Standing in front of the mirror, he ties his tie, noting that he needs a haircut. He tosses his clothes into his duffel, glances around for his notebook. He picks it up, and tucks it into his wallet.

Traffic is heavy on Stadium Boulevard. He stops at the light, gets into the left-hand lane, remembering Stan's assessment of Ann Arbor's road management. *Gotta get those professors humming on this.*

Faber is waiting for him in the lobby of head-quarters, pacing up and down.

"I've been thinking," he says. "I don't know if this is such a great idea."

"Suit yourself." Hugh shrugs. A refusal to cooperate might not be the worst thing at this point.

"On the other hand—they don't make mistakes. Do they?"

"Not that I ever heard of."

"So it'll be the best way to clear my name."

"Absolutely."

The lab room is merely a large closet at the end of the hallway. Hugh opens the door, and the young woman seated behind the table looks up. He introduces himself and she stands to extend her hand.

"Sheila Wells."

She gives James Faber a friendly smile. "Have a seat."

"You say it isn't blood I'm giving?" Faber asks. Evidently he has checked it out ahead of time.

"That's right. They're called buccal samples. It's less invasive. You'll see."

She quickly removes two cotton-tipped applicators from their sterile packaging. "Open your mouth, please."

In seconds she has gently stroked the insides of Faber's cheeks and secured the swabs inside their narrow paper envelopes. Carefully she seals them closed.

"That's it?" Faber asks.

"That's it."

Afterward, Hugh walks him back to the lobby.

"It takes a little while," he says. "I'll drop them off at the lab today."

"What's a little while? Two weeks? A month?"

"Possibly."

"So I'm on file for all time now," Faber says. "Strange feeling. You'll let me know, I assume."

"I will," says Hugh. They have reached the outer doors, where the sunlight streams in through the glass. Hugh watches Faber as he walks briskly toward the tan Mercedes parked out front: brand-spanking clean. Do all executives of the world get their cars washed on Monday mornings?

Faber slides in behind the wheel, looking slim and elegant in his tan suit. *Like a goddamn Good Humor man.* Hugh is grinning as he walks down the hall to thank Sheila Wells for her help. The swabs in their sealed envelopes are tucked inside his breast pocket. One more to go and he can head home. His cell phone rings. He has told Karen to call him if she needs anything picked up.

"Hugh, my friend," Kevin says. "Are you sitting down?"

"What is it?" An arrow of foreboding, but he

dismisses it; these days Kevin's voice is always grim.

"I'm over at Challenge Press," Kevin says. "My guys got a call from the secretary while they were waiting outside."

"What's up?" The arrow is in his gut now. *This can't be happening. It wouldn't make any sense.* But he already knows what it is; he stands still in the hallway, shielding his eyes with his palm, as if to lessen the blow.

"We got here five minutes ago," Kevin says. "I'm in Frisch's office right now. The guy just blew his brains out."

FULL CIRCLE

HE PUT IT TO his right ear and pulled the trigger. Amazing it didn't send him flying. Leg must've caught in the chair." Kevin hands Hugh a note sealed in a bag. He can read it through the clear plastic:

> *I am a liar and a cheat. I am a*
> *crook, but I am not a murderer. I did*
> *not kill Edward Norbois and his*
> *family.*
> *R. H. Frisch*

"Nice penmanship," Kevin says. "It was underneath the In box. Guess he didn't want it to get dirty."

The room itself looks serene and tidy. Except for the body sprawled across the desk. Except for the blood and brain matter slipping down the side of the oak desk and pooling on the floor. Frisch's hand is curled around a 9mm Glock.

Kevin shakes his head. "Why is it the bad guys have all the good guns?"

"It's the wrong gun," Hugh says.

"Yeah. I suppose he didn't want to make things too easy for you. Secretary said he came in this morning very relaxed and calm, told her he had some business to finish up. Closed the door. Next thing she knew: kaboom. Our boys followed him to work. They were right outside the whole time."

"This doesn't make sense," Hugh says. "I saw him last night. I talked him into giving me a DNA sample. He was meeting me this morning at the lab. Ten o'clock . . ."

"Maybe that was it. Anyway, something tipped him over. Could be he and the wife had a fight last night, who knows?"

The wife. The perp. The victim. Another way of keeping things impersonal. Hugh takes in the details of the room—the blotter neatly squared to the desk; pens and pencils in a leather holder; next to it, a photograph of Frisch's wife and two sons. The telephone messages are carefully stacked in a pile.

"You won't have any trouble getting the sample now," Kevin says. Hugh hands the note back, but Kevin waves it away. "No, it's yours. This is still your case. I called the techs. They'll be here any minute. Got a couple of our guys talking with the employees. They're plenty shook. You might want to give Mrs. Ransome a few minutes of your time."

Hugh leaves the room and goes to the secretary's desk. She sits rigidly in her chair, staring at her hands while a young cop bends over her. She looks up at Hugh: "I tried to call you first, Sheriff DeWitt. There was no answer . . ."

"I'm sorry. Are you okay?" She doesn't look it; her face is absolutely gray, and her hands are twisted together in her lap. The cop steps away and he moves in to take his place.

"It'll be all right," he says. Somehow it sounds ridiculous.

Taking a sip of water from a glass on her desk, she sets it down carefully.

"He didn't seem nervous or upset to you?" Hugh asks. "He didn't say or do anything unusual . . . ?"

"He seemed just fine," she says. "Just the same. Nothing was different." She clears her throat. "He asked me to hold his calls. Just for a few minutes, he said. I told him I would. I asked if he wanted me to bring in the mail, and he said not just yet." Her hands clench convulsively in her lap. "Someone should call his wife . . ."

"It's all taken care of," Hugh says. "Mrs. Ransome, you need to go home. Get some rest. This has been a shock."

"No. There are things to be done. Edward would want me to take charge. I've always done that for him." She sags against the chair. "I don't believe this is happening," she says, her voice suddenly high and wooden.

Hugh moves away from the desk, calling the young cop over. "Somebody needs to call Mrs. Ransome's daughter. She needs to get out of here."

———

"Jesus, how'd this happen?" Ian says when Hugh calls the office. "What was he thinking? Were we that close to making an arrest? What should I tell these reporters? They're hanging around here waiting for an update."

"My guess is there'll be a news conference down here this afternoon. Tell them what happened and say that's all you know. What's going on up there?"

"Fredda says Coby and Harmon keep calling,

wanting to know when they can get their guns back."

Hugh laughs grimly. "That's what I need," he says. "Comic relief."

The news conference is brief, and Hugh and Kevin attend it together. Hugh explains that Roger Hamilton Frisch, Comptroller and Acting CEO of Challenge Press, committed suicide in his office at nine-seventeen this morning, July 30. The questions begin before he has time to complete his statement.

"So it's true that Frisch was to be indicted for the murders of Edward Norbois and his family?"

"No, that's not true," Hugh says.

"But he *was* the chief suspect?"

"There are no real suspects yet. The investigation is still in the preliminary stages. We're following up on several leads," Hugh says, "but there's no reason to assume at this point that Mr. Frisch's suicide is connected to the Norbois murders, other than in a peripheral way."

"—Will they be releasing the bodies soon?"

"—Have the autopsies been completed?"

"—There's a rumor it may have been two shooters. Could you comment on that, Sheriff?"

"—What's the story on company funds being embezzled?"

"—What about the forged checks? Was Frisch responsible for that?"

"Whew!" Hugh loosens his collar as he and Kevin leave the steps and walk back through headquarters.

"Yeah. You get used to it after a while. Main thing to remember is not to let them get you mad. And don't ever ask them where they got anything. Makes 'em look smarter than you."

"I do wonder how they found out about the forged checks."

"Who knows?" Kevin shrugs. "They're like moles. Always be straight with them if you can. They get nasty if they think you're holding back." He looks at Hugh. "Where you headed now?"

"Grand Rapids. I want to get these samples over to Blodgett Hospital."

"Samples? More than one?"

"I took one from James Faber. The broker who was having an affair with Mrs. Norbois."

"Looks to me like Roger Frisch was dead meat before the suicide," Kevin says. "You think this is coincidence? One day he's caught with his hand in the till. He's going to end up in jail. The next day, his boss gets gunned down. Now there's a piece of bad luck for you."

"It doesn't make sense to me that the whole

family gets blown away over a white-collar crime. Why not just wait and catch Norbois in a dark alley some night, make it look like a robbery?"

"Hughie, I should only be this lucky. The guy's guilty. He commits suicide because he can't take the pressure. He killed six innocent people . . ." Kevin throws up his hands. "Okay, do what you have to. Check Faber's DNA. Check everybody's in the world if you want. Only don't be surprised when Frisch's tests come back positive."

"Kev, I appreciate the advice," Hugh says carefully, "but I'm not sure I buy that." He wants it to sound neutral, but he hears it coming out less than graceful. He *is* annoyed about Kevin's resources being spread so thin. It would help a lot to have some of the more minor tasks taken off his hands. But they are friends. And they are both under a ton of pressure. Who knows? They could be out on their asses after this next election. Not that this would be the worst thing, in Hugh's opinion; no, the worst thing would be not solving this crime to his own satisfaction. Not being able to give this family justice.

———

"Hey, it's my pal Hughie!" Billy Shaw opens the door to his office in Blodgett Hospital. "Welcome to the Sanctum Sanctorum."

"Let me tell you about my lousy day," Hugh says.

"Yeah. I saw you on TV. You're one tight-lipped dude."

"Bugger off," Hugh says, handing over the serology carton and the two sealed envelopes.

"Heard the latest?" Billy asks. "Report's back on the fourth coed. She was raped. DNA's the same as in the other three women."

"That was quick."

"Yeah, we got his DNA blueprint memorized. I can almost see the sorry little bastard coming with the naked eye."

"You going to release it to the newspapers?"

Billy shakes his head. "I like to wait till I'm asked. I sent the stuff on to Chief Watkins. He can do the honors. What have you got for me?"

"Blood samples from Roger Frisch's body. Plus buccal cells from a James Faber."

"Who's he?"

"Stockbroker who knew Paige Norbois."

"I assume in the biblical sense."

"Right. I figure if I can eliminate these guys as the rapist, I eliminate them as the killer as well."

Billy grins. "Two for the price of one. Save you the trouble, though; stockbrokers don't do murder, they just lose money for people."

"How long will it take, d'you think?"

"Ha. I know you detective types, you're like

movie people. You want everything yesterday. I can imagine how you feel, though."

"I don't think you can, Billy."

"The way this coed killer keeps hiding these bodies," Billy says, "you know what I think? I think he wants to come back and take another look when he feels like it. This last one, he was just unlucky. Her body might not have surfaced for two or three months if those kids hadn't stumbled over it."

"Yeah, well, I'd love to stay and chat," Hugh says. "After today I don't feel like talking about dead bodies, hidden or otherwise."

"I'll get back to you as quick as I can," Billy says. "I know I've got the LaChappelle boys pending, too."

"Maybe you'll give me a deal on multiple submissions."

"Hugh, are you okay?"

"Yeah, I'm fine."

"You don't sound fine," Karen says. "I saw the news conference. Fredda called to tell me."

He makes a face, looking at himself in the bathroom mirror. He has just arrived at the motel, after a stop at a small burger joint north of Ann Arbor. He doesn't want to tell Karen the amount of pure grease he just ate. It sits at the bottom of his stomach like lead.

"Becky wants to say 'hi,'" Karen says.

"Daddy, I thought you were coming home!"

"Me, too, hon. I'm sorry I won't be able to drive you up to camp."

"It's okay. I saw you on TV. So did Donna and Isabel. They thought you looked cute."

"They've seen me before."

"Yeah, but it's different when you're on TV. Daddy, I read something about the murder of that family up here. What does it mean, the bodies were beyond recognition?"

He winces. "They'd been dead for a while, hon. Things start to decay . . ."

"Joanna says it means they were like mush. And that they smelled like that dead deer we found in the woods last year. Yuk. Listen, will you be able to come for the gymkhana? It's at the end of camp."

He's still back with the bodies looking like mush. How is she able to make these leaps? Never mind, more power to her. "For sure I will. Now you be extra careful, will you?"

"Daddy," she says patiently. "Remember: *'Don't worry about what might happen, just worry about what does.'*"

Good grief. Now his ten-year-old daughter is giving him counsel; things have come to a pretty pass.

"Two whole weeks with you gone at camp," he says. "How am I going to survive?"

There's a smirk in her voice: "Oh, you'll manage. I feel sorrier for Mom. She's the one who has to do everything."

"What does that mean?" he asks when Karen gets back on the phone.

She laughs. "I guess it means she misses you. We both do. We're eating like pigs over here," she says. "Big, slobbery pigs."

"You trying to turn me on, or what?"

She is silent a moment. Then: "Hugh, why did Frisch do this?"

"I wish I knew."

"It sure makes him look guilty, doesn't it?"

"Yeah, but I don't believe it. Somehow it feels too pat."

"What does Kevin think?"

"Kevin thinks case closed. Keep it simple, stupid."

"Does it remind you of the Leyden case?" she asks. "Remember? That family that was killed up in Bay View?"

"Yeah, I remember. Guy who fought with all of his neighbors and treated his employees like dirt. Everyone thought the family was killed because of him."

"Yes," she says. "Only it turned out his wife was having an affair with the choir director at church. And she was about to confess it to the minister. So the choir director shot them all."

"And your point is . . . ?" Hugh asks.

"Support for your theory," Karen says. "The most obvious suspect isn't always the killer. And the most obvious victim isn't always the source of the crime."

"I think that was last week's theory."

"You have good instincts, Hugh. If it doesn't feel right to you, it's probably not right."

"Karey," he says, "the truth is, I'm burning out here. Not just on this case."

Her voice is suddenly very businesslike. "You always say that. On every case."

"You're kidding me."

"No. It's just the way you are until you come up with the right answer." She takes a breath. "However. I also think you have a lot on your mind these days."

"You do, huh?"

"Yes. And I don't think it has anything to do with burning out on the job."

He laughs. "Now there's a meal. Don't give me too much to chew on."

"I love you," she says.

"Love you, too."

"Hugh? Don't overlook the beautiful people. That choir director was a very beautiful man. It doesn't mean he wasn't a killer. Now get some sleep."

"Okay." He hangs up, smiling. She always knows how to turn his mood around. Stretching out on the bed, he reaches over to the nightstand for the remote. This place has cable TV; instead of lying here wide awake, he might just take the evening off and watch *Sex and the City*.

TWO FUNERALS

As Hugh suspected, the Maasso Funeral Chapel is jammed with friends, neighbors, and business associates of the Norbois family—all outnumbered, of course, by the catastrophe junkies. He will never understand how otherwise normal people crave this hit from an encounter with the macabre.

Well, they won't be getting it here. Nothing is even mentioned about the manner of death, other than a brief reference to "circumstances beyond our control." No caskets, either; only engraved

funeral cards stating that the ashes of the family
will be scattered at a later date.

Edwin Norbois's cousin, Amelia Navarro,
stands, like a sentry, at the end of the narrow
viewing room. When Hugh met her yesterday at
Kevin's office, she was quick to inform him that
she and the other cousins—Francis and Douglas
Norbois—would be attending the services as a
courtesy to the deceased. "We weren't close, you
know. We barely knew them." They were also in
town for the reading of the will.

Amelia Navarro had her own opinion of the
case, which coincided with Kevin's. "It would
seem you needn't look further than a crooked
business partner with a grudge." It would seem,
also, that he should know a lot about them—that
their great-grandfather, Eaton Norbois, was a
lumber baron who owned a chain of sawmills on
Lake Huron. That his name was on the
Lumberman's Monument, on the River Road outside Oscoda. When Hugh admitted he'd never
seen the monument, all three eyed him with dis-
dain. What kind of sheriff was he? Some know-
nothing hick, no doubt.

Bulletin boards with family pictures are sta-
tioned in strategic areas of the room, together
with a number of floral tributes. It occurs to Hugh
this has taken a fair amount of organization; he
wonders who's responsible for it. Surely not these

cousins. *Blood will tell,* Hugh thinks. If people thought Edward a cold fish, they should only meet his relatives.

———

Thank God the room is air-conditioned. Everyone here is dressed in the lightest of attire, and still the place seems stuffy. There's a hum of barely concealed tension in the air. Hugh sees Elaine and Matt Spiteri standing with James Faber at the end of the room; all three look unhappy.

"They could've at least said something at the service," Elaine is saying as Hugh walks up.

"Hullo, DeWitt," Matt says. "Just ripping up the relatives to pass the time."

Elaine presses a restraining hand against his arm.

"So, what's your take on this latest development?" Faber asks Hugh. "Frisch's suicide, I mean. I guess this pretty much wraps things up, huh?"

"Could be," says Hugh.

"Why not make an announcement?" Matt says. "That's what all the ghouls and vultures are waiting for. I hear the trio of cousins will inherit everything."

"That's the rumor," Hugh says.

"Seems like they could at least shed a tear or two at the festivities."

"Oh, *please,*" says Elaine.

It dawns on Hugh that both Matt Spiteri and James Faber have been drinking. Across the room the Norbois cousins are glancing at their respective watches. For once Hugh is in sympathy. He notices a young, dark-haired woman making her way purposefully toward him.

"Excuse me," he says, happy to be free of the Spiteris' edgy dynamic. And what the hell is up with Faber? No doubt he's starting to regret having given up the DNA sample. *Let them stew,* he thinks.

The young woman is holding out her hand: "My name is Gina Keyes," she says. "Derek Norbois and I were friends. We lived in the same rooming house." Her breath catches. "This is just so terrible . . . Derek was such a good guy, so funny . . . we used to hang out together during football season. We'd sit on the porch drinking beer . . ."

He ushers her across the room. "I think I've seen some sketches Derek did of you," he says.

She nods. "He was always drawing. It was the only thing he cared about."

"When was the last time you saw him?"

"It was in March," she says. "Right before I moved out. I left when that girl who lived across the street from us was killed. Camilla Reusse. My roommate and I decided to find another apartment."

Camilla Reusse. He remembers her name from

the newspaper article. "She lived across the street from the rooming house?" he asks.

"Yes. It just . . . it didn't feel safe there anymore. We just couldn't stay."

"Did you know Camilla Reusse?"

"No, but Derek did. They were friends. He went out with her a few times. I know he was pretty shook up after she was . . . after she died."

"I take it you didn't have any trouble breaking your lease."

"No. We split the difference with Maura. The place is a rat trap, anyway, and she knows it."

Hugh takes out his card, hands it to the young woman. "I'd like to talk to you again, Gina. I'd appreciate it if you'd give me your number."

"Sure." She jots it down on the card.

———

A group of teenagers are standing by the door of the chapel; Hugh recognizes two of them as girls whose pictures were on Steve Norbois's dresser. One of them wipes her fingers under her brimming eyes. The boy next to her tells Hugh that his aunt owns a cabin in Cross Village.

"I used to run into Steve and Derek up there once in a while," he says.

"Do you happen to know if they ever hung out with any of the local kids?" Hugh asks.

"Yeah, Steve did. A guy named Denny Maillot. I met him once at a beach party. But I don't stay around much on weekends. It's pretty dead at night. We usually mosey over to Charlevoix if we want some live action."

Denny Maillot. Herb Maillot's kid. At least one OUIL in his high school career. So he and Stephen Norbois were friends. Like evidently attracts like.

———

Clouds threaten overhead when Hugh arrives at the Kingsley Funeral Chapel. They won't amount to anything, though. The leaves on the trees hang limply in the dead air.

The number of cars in the parking lot reflects the half-empty chapel; the services were not announced in the newspaper. Valerie Frisch sits alone in the front row next to her two small sons, the casket mounted on a low platform before them. The service is blessedly short, conducted by a man in a long white robe and dark socks with sandals, who talks in a nearly inaudible whisper. Hugh, seated at the back, can barely hear him.

". . . entered into the world with no misgivings . . . faith in God . . . he knew his Redeemer . . ." Thus, with a handful of generic phrases, Roger Frisch is laid to rest.

"Thank you for coming," Valerie Frisch says as Hugh comes up to take her hand. She clutches a handkerchief in her fist but she is smiling faintly; the black dress seems reminiscent of cocktail party attire. Hugh feels a flash of annoyance, even as his heart contracts with pity. Valerie Frisch seems more ill-at-ease than genuinely sad. When he spoke to her the other day to secure her permission for Frisch's blood sample, he'd seen a look on her face that reminded him of Becky—a look she wore when she hurt herself in some careless accident and was trying not to cry.

Now Valerie Frisch says to him: "I'd like to talk to you, if you could stop over at the house tonight." She glances at her two boys, standing apart from her in the doorway. "Just a minute." She walks away to confer with a woman across the room. In a moment she's back. "We can do it here actually," she says. "If you have time. People will be leaving soon."

"Sure. That's fine."

He wanders the halls of the chapel, studying the paintings on the walls, of clouds drifting over serene country settings and hills dappled with golden light. Everything fairylike and unreal. He remembers pacing the halls of the Carlisle Funeral Chapel after Petey died; the pictures there had the same feeling of irrelevance. What he wanted was dark, roiling landscapes, full of fury and vengeance.

He hears footsteps behind him, turns around.

"I've sent the kids on home," Valerie Frisch says. "We can use the office at the end of the hall."

She takes his arm, leading him into the small room and closing the door. Sitting down in one of the chairs, she wipes her eyes with her handkerchief. "God, how could he do this to me? How could he leave me with this *mess?*"

"I'm sorry . . ." Hugh says.

"That day he left . . ." She blows her nose, pockets the handkerchief, and looks up at him. ". . . I don't understand . . . I mean I knew he was depressed. But that wasn't anything new. He was a manic-depressive. He was on lithium. He's been on it for years . . ."

"Did you know he had embezzled money from the company?" Hugh asks her gently.

"Of course I knew," she snaps. "I knew about everything. The forged checks. All of it. He would have returned it all . . ." Her voice trails off. ". . . but the money kept disappearing. It was . . . like it was running downhill. And he couldn't stop it." She squares her shoulders, sitting up straight. "That money was just sitting there. Not being used, not helping anyone. That's what Rog believed, that money should help people. The more it circulates, the more people will benefit from it. He wasn't a greedy person, he was an idealist. He gave money to the church, to people in need . . . he was generous, caring . . ."

"But you knew what he was doing was illegal," Hugh says.

"Yes, I knew. And we both knew he had to return it before anyone found out. And he would have . . . he had a plan . . . but then everything fell apart." She clears her throat. "He was resigned to the fact that he'd probably lose his job. Rog was a brilliant man. He *never* had trouble getting a job. We were figuring out where we'd go from here . . . when this awful thing with the Norbois family happened." She looks up at Hugh. "Edward didn't tolerate mistakes very well. One wrong turn and he wiped your slate clean of the good stuff. Very little praise. Lots of blame."

"I take it you didn't like him much."

"Oh, Edward wasn't a man you liked or disliked. I didn't know him well enough for that. Nobody really knew him. But he and Rog were alike in some ways. They were both very lonely men." Again, she looks directly at him. "Rog would never do a thing like those murders. He was an *injured* person. It took everything he had *every day* just to go out into the world. He was terrified all the time."

"Terrified of what?"

"Of *life!*" She shrugs her shoulders. "Just . . .

living." She pinches the bridge of her nose. "We never had any secrets from each other. That's why I have to know what happened, why he did this. Killed himself, I mean."

"Where was he on the afternoon of the twenty-fifth?" Hugh asks. "He didn't go to the convention, did he?"

"No. He was upset about Edward's phone call. He told me about it later. He didn't go to Cobo Hall. He went to the woods. That's what he did when things were bad . . . he'd go for a walk in the woods. He said it helped him, to see the way nature endures. He has a special place, out near Pinckney on the Potawatomi Trail. He can be there for hours and never see a single soul."

"So," Hugh says. "He had no alibi for that day."

"That's right."

"And you were home by nine o'clock that night and he was there when you came in."

"Yes." She keeps looking at him, and he feels a rush of pain, a connection with her so strong it nearly takes his breath away. She reaches out to put a hand on his arm; her grip is surprisingly powerful. "I think I know why. I think he couldn't stand the shame of it. Watching his kids suffer, even though he was innocent. That's why he killed himself. There would always be this stigma."

Hugh stands up. Things are tipping into overload; selfishly, he'd like to get out of here before it happens.

"We were *helpmates*," she says. "I want to clear his name. I can at least do that much for him."

TIES THAT BIND

"Got a minute?" Hugh asks.

"Got a warrant?" Maura grins. She opens her apartment door to admit him. She's dressed in a different black outfit today—a sleeveless dress that hangs demurely from her shoulders. Her feet are clad in black ballet slippers. A strip of fuchsia silk is wound around her head. Black must be the uniform of choice. Glancing toward the oak armoire, Hugh imagines it loaded with clothes of this color. As if reading his mind, Maura asks: "Want to take a look inside?"

He smiles. "I'd rather talk. Clear up a few things."

"Clear away, then."

"How was it left with you and Derek?"

"About what?"

"About whether or not he'd be living here in the fall."

"I told him if he wanted a room, the best way would be to pay rent through the summer. He didn't offer to do it, so I assumed he wasn't planning on coming back."

"Did it have anything to do with Camilla Reusse having been killed?"

"Why would it?"

"Because a couple of your other tenants moved out after it happened."

"Who told you that?" She shrugs her shoulders. "They were infants. She didn't die because she lived across the street from me, she died because she went to a beer party in Delhi Park. I told them that's what they should stay away from."

"Were you aware that Derek and Camilla Reusse were friends?"

"I saw him walk her home once. Listen, I was his *landlady*. Besides, Derek wasn't much of a talker."

"You're not, either," he says. "Why didn't you tell me you and he had dated?"

She laughs outright. "*Dated.* Now there's a hip

term. Why didn't you ask me? We fucked a few times, yes."

Despite her defiance, he can't help admiring her; she's not about to be pushed around by tough talk, even when it comes from a cop. He wonders how often she's had to protect herself in this way. He tries to soften his manner: "Do you know if anybody here carries a weapon?"

"In this house, you mean? Sure. Every woman I know. They've all got Swiss Army knives. It only makes sense, after what happened."

"I was thinking about guns," he says.

"You mean, besides me?" Moving to a drawer in the counter she opens it and pushes aside some dishtowels. She pulls out a small handgun.

"Mind if I take a look at it?"

"It isn't loaded." She hands it over and he hefts it, looking down the barrel. J. P. Sauer & Sohn Suhl. Cal 7.65 mm. The European equivalent of an American .32.

"Nice weapon. Where'd you get it?"

"From my uncle," she says. "He thought I needed it."

"What for?"

"When I make my deposits at the bank. I take it with me. Just to be on the safe side. Are you wondering if it's registered? Because it is."

Hugh hands it back to her. "And your registration allows you to carry it on your person?"

"Right. You can check that out with the Ann
Arbor police if you want."

———

Guy Mason is working on a green Honda motorcycle out in the yard as Hugh leaves the building.

"Hey. The sheriff. How's it going?"

"Good," Hugh says. "How's it with you?"

"Okay, except I got a bad O-ring. Should've
taken care of it at the shop. So what were you
talking to my landlady about?"

"Just routine," Hugh says. "I've been thinking
about what you said about joining the force. Were
you serious?"

"Yeah, I think I was. What do I have to do?"

"Depends. You interested in evidence technol-
ogy? That's the field now. There's a good school
right here in Ann Arbor." Hugh reaches into his
pocket for Kevin's card. "I got you the name of
someone who'll help you through the hoops."

Guy takes the card from him. "Hey, the chief
of police. I'm impressed."

"Yeah, we went to school together." Hugh
bends down to check out the Honda. "I didn't
know you owned a motorcycle."

"Yeah, I got two more back there in the shed.
My mom says, 'What's the sense in that? You can
only ride one at a time.'"

"I used to be a motorcycle cop," Hugh says.

"No kidding."

"I didn't like it, though. Too dangerous. My mom didn't much like it either. Listen," Hugh says, "I was hoping you could help me out with something. Have you got a few minutes? We'd need to take a trip across town."

"Sure thing." Guy stands up, wiping his hands on a towel. "Where are we going? To the station house?"

"No. The Norbois place."

"Let me get my smokes." He wheels the bike around to the back of the house while Hugh waits in the yard. He glances up at Maura's window, but there's no sign of life. Does she know that he's still out here? *She must.*

Guy reappears wearing a clean shirt, with his hair neatly combed. He walks with Hugh toward the patrol car.

"Never been inside one of these before. Lots of hi-tech gizmos, huh?"

"Gizmos galore," Hugh agrees. "Make yourself at home."

"What's this?" Guy points to the Remington 870 mounted between the seats.

"Shotgun."

"So do you two guys talk over cases with each other?" he asks. "You and Chief Watkins?"

"Sometimes."

"Where'd you go to cop school?"

"Michigan State."

Guy reaches down to adjust the passenger seat. "You like the Crown Victoria? Is it a good driving car?"

"It's okay," Hugh says. "I'm not a car guy, though."

Guy grins. "I thought all cops were car guys."

"Well, there's your prejudice showing."

Guy opens the window. "Mind if I smoke?"

"No, go ahead."

He takes a pack of Marlboros from his shirt pocket. "I've been trying to quit. My mom's on me about it all the time. She works at a nursing home where half the people are dying of emphysema." He lights up, looking for the ashtray.

"Right here." Hugh shows him. "You and your mom are pretty tight, I take it."

"I guess. My dad took off when I was two. She's had to work pretty hard."

"You her only kid?"

"Yeah. Here, take Washtenaw. That's the fastest way over there."

"I need to grab something to eat first. Haven't eaten all day. I'll buy you a burger."

"So this is how it works, huh?" Guy leans back in his seat. "You pull something out of a hat and just go with it."

"That's how it's done. You tend to find a lot of answers by accident."

"I like the sound of that. What else do I need to know about being a cop?"

"Keep your options open. And try not to miss what's right in front of you." Hugh turns into the Burger King parking lot at the corner of Washtenaw and State and places their order, then pulls ahead to the pickup window. "I've noticed," he says, "that Derek Norbois drew a lot of pictures of women."

"Yeah. They were his favorite subject. Kind of odd, considering how clueless he was with 'em in real life."

"Not like you, huh?"

Guy grins. "Nothing like me."

"You think there's a possibility he was gay?"

"Derek? Nah. He liked girls; he just didn't have any inkling of how to deal with them. Sometimes it took the girls a while to get it. No moves can sometimes be mistaken for big, fancy moves."

Hugh laughs. "I've been looking through his sketches," he says, "trying to figure something out. Why there are no pictures of Camilla Reusse."

Guy frowns. "I know that name. That's the girl who lived across the street from us. The one who was killed back in March."

"Right. Evidently she and Derek were friends."

"I never met her." Guy shrugs. "Can't figure out how I missed her, either. She was a looker, from the pictures I saw in the paper."

———

Hugh parks in the driveway of the Norbois house, leading the way through the door inside the garage.

"This house," Guy says, "always blows my mind. It's so damned huge."

"Were you over here a lot?" Hugh asks.

"A few times." He looks around. "I read in the paper it's worth a million bucks."

"At least."

They walk up the wide staircase together and enter Derek's bedroom. Hugh goes to the bed, where the drawings are scattered about. Guy remains standing in the doorway, hands in his pockets.

"Here's what I'd like you to do," Hugh says. "Identify as many people in these sketches as you can."

"He drew a lot of people. He was drawing all the time."

"I know. Just do your best."

"I didn't think it'd feel this weird," Guy says, after a moment. "Being back in this house. After all that's happened." He moves slowly toward the bed.

"Yeah, it gives one pause," says Hugh. "It looks to me like he did sketches of just about everyone he knew. The women, at least."

"He sure drew plenty of our landlady," Guy says. "Where's the one of her in her bikini?" He riffles through the sketches, coming up with a charcoal drawing and handing it to Hugh. "Here it is."

Hugh stares down at the tight, spare lines. Maura James lies on the lawn in the backyard, a hand propping her head, looking over her shoulder at him. The graceful curve of her bare back ends in a smudgy triangle; her free hand trails languidly in the grass.

"That's one he drew of her right after he moved in," Guy says.

"Was that when they were together?"

"I wouldn't call it being together, exactly." Guy grins. "It's hard to keep up with Maura's love life. She was always busy."

"Was she busy with you, too?"

"Oh, sure. A couple of years ago. Now it's pretty much cash and carry. She gets a little testy when you owe her money."

"Have you ever met this uncle of hers?" Hugh asks.

"A couple of times, yeah. Seems like an okay

guy. Her old man is one step away from being a street bum, though. Her mom finally shook him off, but he stumbles over to the house every so often looking for a handout from Maura."

"That's tough."

"Yeah, but she's a tough cookie." Guy shrugs. "And I guess everybody's got their skeletons. So what do you think will happen to all this stuff?"

"Hard to say. The estate owns it now."

"Too bad," Guy says. "I think Derek could've become famous. He's a damned good artist, don't you think?"

"There are lots of good artists in the world," Hugh says. "The sad fact is, most of them don't become famous."

"One thing I should tell you," Guy says on the way back to the apartment building. "I don't much like guns. You think that'll be a problem? If I decide to be a cop?"

Hugh shakes his head. "Most people are afraid of guns until they learn how to handle them. That's what they teach you at the academy. Anyway, being a cop isn't all about shooting a gun."

"Good. That's what I was hoping to hear. Thanks for the heads-up. I'll call this guy tomorrow."

Hugh drops Guy off, then drives down State

Street and parks on Thayer, behind the Women's League. He feels suddenly exhausted, and a strange brightness is pressing against his eyes; he tries to blink it away. He'd love to be home with nothing but a quiet evening ahead of him—watering Karen's garden, or sitting with Becky while she's recounting her day. But he doesn't believe that Blessed misses him as much as he misses Blessed. And that's another sad fact.

He reaches under the front seat, pulling out the supply of plastic bags he keeps there. Dropping Guy's empty Coke cup into one bag and sealing it closed, he then empties the ashtray, seals it into another bag, and clips the two together. *Keeping his options open. Trying not to miss what's right in front of him.*

FALLING INTO PLACE

THE FRONT DOOR opens as Hugh pulls into the driveway. He climbs out of the car and Karen puts her arms around him; he presses his face against her hair.

"How was the drive?"

"Not bad. How are the horses?"

"Oh, she's happy as can be. She wants to live there. She thinks we should buy her one for her birthday."

They both laugh. "Lucky we don't have any money."

"Are you hungry? There's some cold beef in the refrige."

"Nah. Let's just have a drink." He sinks down on the couch, slipping his shoes off. "Feels like a month since I've been home. What day is it anyway?"

"It's the fifth."

"Of August? Or September?"

Karen laughs. She goes to the kitchen while he sits, arms along the back of the couch, staring wearily into space. Now that he's here, what next? He needed to get out of Ann Arbor—just for a break—but he left a flood of unanswered questions.

What was it that Faber said to him? *I'm on file for all time now.* Something about that comment doesn't sit right. Maybe just the timing of it—his finding out about Frisch's suicide only moments later. But now he doesn't trust the guy, even as he feels a certain kinship with him; they have both lost only sons, a fact that seems to connect them in some profound way. What did Faber say at the funeral? *I guess this pretty much wraps things up.* So damned sure of himself he is.

Still, the money is on Roger Frisch. Unless his DNA doesn't show up in Paige's and Nicole's bodies. Whoever raped them has got to be the murderer. And what if it turns out that it isn't either Frisch *or* Faber? What then? Hugh remembers his dad once telling him that there are cases that give you an overload of clues: *too many facets; not enough facts.*

Karen returns with his drink. "Here you go. Scotch on the rocks."

"Thanks. What are you having?"

"Just water. It's late. I'd be up all night. So tell me what's been going on down there in the last week."

"I have a hunch it was the wife's lover," he says. Amazed at the firmness of the statement. *Is* that what he thinks, then? "He's so damned slick. With his coffee-colored suit that matches his coffee-colored Mercedes."

"Ah. And is he good-looking, too?"

He laughs. "Jesus, am I that shallow?"

"You're that tired," she says, slipping an arm through his and caressing his wrist. "Let's go upstairs. I'll tell you everything I've been doing while you've been gone."

"Did you paint the bathroom?" he asks as they climb the stairs. "Whatever it is, I'll bet it's going to cost me money . . ."

Her body next to his feels firm, almost like a boy's; no extra cushioning anywhere. It suddenly dawns on him that she's losing weight. How could he not have noticed this?

"Hey, what's going on? You're so thin."

"Hughie. Relax. I'm fine. Everything's fine. You're in Distress Mode."

Once in the bedroom, they undress silently, and Karen moves toward him. He sits down on the bed, shifting his weight to receive her as she kneels between his legs.

"Needles and pins, needles and pins . . ." he hums to himself. ". . . when a man marries, his trouble begins."

"Oh, that's nice. Who said that?"

"My mom."

Karen laughs. "I always knew she was twisted."

He leans over to kiss the soft skin of her stomach. "Don't be after me, now," he growls. "I'm whacked . . ."

Her hands brush lightly across his groin, and it's all that is needed; his stomach contracts in dizzying ecstasy, and he is *there,* lying on his back, ready for her, arms stretched above his head.

"I missed you . . ." She presses herself tight against him; a slippery slickness between them as she readies herself to take him inside. And a split-second later the feeling passes, everything passes; his cock is soft, flabby, limp against his groin.

"Shit," he murmurs in weary despair. "What is the fucking deal?"

"My fault." She reaches for his hand.

"Jesus. Okay. It's your fault."

"I just meant . . . this is what happens when things move too fast. After we've been apart. It's nothing new."

"Yeah, same old, same old."

"Hughie, listen. Everything's okay. We're okay. I'm not worried."

"Right," he says. "You're not worried. That's terrific." But he pulls her down on top of him so that her head rests against his shoulder. "I'm sorry, Karey."

"It's not the end of the world," she says. "I just want you here. I don't care."

"Yeah. Me neither. Let's just go to sleep." He is suddenly exhausted, too tired to move. He will lie here until he can summon up enough energy to get under the covers.

"On the other hand," she says. "We could talk about it."

Inwardly he groans, wrapping her more tightly in his arms.

"I just wish you would go see Doc DeVere. It's probably some simple thing that can be fixed."

"Yeah, and what if it isn't?"

"Don't you want to find out?"

"No."

"Liar." She raises up and he recognizes this as the opening signal of a lecture. "You're a perfectly normal thirty-eight-year-old who happens to live a very stressful life. It's not all that uncommon."

"You know this for a fact."

"I've heard it."

"From who?"

"Don't change the subject. And, anyway, I care about this because you care."

"Look, let's just table it for now, okay? I'll get it figured out. I promise."

"You've been promising," she says, "for a while now."

"Okay! Look. I can't just drop everything right now." He rolls to his side. "I can't ignore all this. Just because you want to get pregnant."

Oh, shit, now where in hell did that come from? He lies there, waiting for some sort of clarification—from whom? Surely not his wife, who has chosen this moment to sit up with her back to him, the polished curve of her neck outlined in the light from the window. Her arms are bent about her raised knees. At last she turns to look at him.

"Is it so damned odd that I might want to have another baby?" she asks. "Is it something we have to tiptoe around for the rest of our lives?"

"That was stupid," he says. "I didn't mean to say that."

"Did you ever think I might want to talk about it? *Okay, I agree, no more kids.* Or *Let's have more kids, just not right now?* Did you ever wonder what Becky might be thinking about it?"

He is silent. Things are suddenly moving too fast for him. Resting a cautious hand on her back, he says: "I'm sorry."

"You brought it up," she says, in a voice so soft he can barely hear it. "So I guess it wasn't such a big secret, after all."

He remembers Kevin's wife, Delia, back during the days when he and Karen were in grief; back when his rage at life, at the mindless cruelty of it, was so immense that it threatened to engulf them: *Don't try to fix it, Hugh. Just listen and try not to say anything stupid.*

"It's all right," Karen says. "Whatever you're feeling. But I need to *know.*"

How can he tell her when he doesn't know himself? He's afraid to utter a word, afraid of saying the wrong thing.

"Because if that's what's making you impotent . . ."

Ay yi yi, does she have to put it like this? Aloud he soothes her: "I love *you,* Karey. I'll talk to Doc DeVere. Tomorrow. I promise."

WHERE RIPENS THE GRAIN

HE ENTERS THE station house through the sally port, to avoid the gaggle of reporters hanging around in the lobby. Fredda smiles as he comes in.

"Sneaky," she says. "Long time no see."

"Did you miss me?"

"It goes without saying."

Ian comes around the corner. "She's been sassing me the whole time you were gone, Hugh. She won't buy that flavored cream for the coffee anymore, either. I say let's get rid of her."

"Yes? And who'd clean up all those funky sentences of yours in the daily reports?" Fredda hands Hugh the telephone messages. He glances down at the top one:

Leonard Warner
555-7892

"Who's this?"

"Guy I told you about," Ian says. "The one who lives out near the Norbois place. I tried to take it, but he only wants to talk to you. Says he knew your dad. Says they went to University of Michigan together."

"Okay. How're you handling the pundits these days?"

"They like me. That is, everybody but Stu Hamilton. He only wants to hear it from you. He says he and your dad went to Michigan together."

"Shut up." He goes into his office and sits down at his desk, dialing Leonard Warner's number.

"This is Sheriff DeWitt."

"Oh, yeah. Thanks for calling back. Say, I think I might have something for you. About the Norbois killings? I overheard two guys talking at the Outback Bar. Maybe it's nothing, but I thought I ought to pass it on. But I'm heading back to Detroit in a couple of hours—"

"I can come out right now," Hugh says.

"Great. We're across from the Teeter place, on the lower road. Just before it turns west—?"

"Yeah, I know Teeters'. I'll be right there."

The old horse farm, which sold to Hy Jensen back in the seventies, is still referred to as the Teeter place by the natives. Leonard Warner isn't a native, he's sure of it; but historic snobbery rules, and it's getting harder to tell the old guard from the *New Voh Reesh,* as Sarah Clement would say.

The Warner house looks modest from the front, but Hugh knows better; these places are monsters, their vast bulk hidden below the steep bluff. This one has a funicular parked alongside, with the scaffolding barely visible through a wall of honeysuckle and lilac. Next to it, the wide deck gives off a spectacular view of the lake and of Beaver Island, that huge, gray whale lying twenty-five miles off the coast.

Leonard Warner is a tall, thin man, distinguished-looking, with gray hair and long, thin hands and feet. He's waiting just inside as Hugh approaches the front door.

"We haven't met," he says, extending his hand. "I knew your dad at Michigan. Helluva good running back. We played on the freshman team together. Never thought he'd end up a cop, though."

Hugh doesn't know what to say to this, merely shakes the man's hand. "You say you've got some information . . . ?"

"Yeah. C'mon inside."

He leads Hugh into the spacious living room with a sliding glass door at the end of it, opening onto a platform. There the railcar sits, ready to ferry passengers to the beach. They cross the white carpeting, and Hugh glances toward the row of windows that fronts the bay, stretching across the length of the room. Below lies a forest of cedars, sloping down to the beach.

"I've seen those guys up at the bar before," Warner is saying. "They both have cottages down the way on the lower road. Couple of shacks is more like it, but they're grandfathered in."

There's a strict demarcation between the two ends of the lower road: the end closer to town and settled earlier is nevertheless considered the inferior direction; the venue of choice is the end where Warner lives.

"I've been up here alone for a week or so," Warner continues. "My wife's down taking care of our daughter. She just had a baby, our thirteenth grandchild. Lucky thirteen. I'm driving down to see them today."

"Who are these men you saw at the Outback?" Hugh asks.

"Names are Joe Dibold and Ray Potts. They

hang out there playing pool and generally acting obnoxious. I was sitting at the bar a couple of weeks ago, watching the Tigers on TV. The place was packed. It was noisy, too. But the pool table's right next to the TV, and all of a sudden I realize these two are talking about the murders. So I start paying attention. They were saying something about 'Little Stevie Wonder'—the Norbois kid—what a prick he was, telling them he was going to call the cops on them. 'Guess he won't be doing that anytime soon,' one of them says. So when I got home that night I got to thinking about it. And I remembered I saw those same two guys on the beach about six weeks ago. They were moving a big hunk of driftwood. I watched them through the binoculars and they walked it through the water, down to where their cottages are.

"I remember it was around six o'clock in the evening, because I was thinking they were smart to pick a time when there's less activity, so they wouldn't have to explain what the hell they were doing."

"Explain . . . ?"

"Yeah. It's against the law, you know. To move a piece of shipwreck. That thing's been down there for years. It's huge—longer than a telephone pole, curved, like a part of a bow. They were dragging it down to their place. The law says you can't move a derelict from its resting place . . ."

"And this was when? Around the end of June?"

Warner moves to the large oak buffet across the room. "Yeah. I was going to call the DNR myself about it, but I never got around to it. And then the other night I looked it up on my calendar." He does this now, flipping through a large daybook lying, open, on the counter. "Here. Come and see."

The daybook, written in several different hands, is the work of an assembly of obsessive diarists. No activity is too small to go unrecorded: *"pick strawberries"*; *"Wares and Byes arrive"*; *"kids to Garden Island"*; *"trip to Georgian Bay"*; *"take Buick in for oil change."*

"See here?" Warner points to the notation on June 25. *"Dibold and Potts move shipwreck."* Isn't that the day of the murders? At least, that's what the papers say . . ."

"Yes," Hugh says. "And this happened at around six o'clock in the evening?"

"Maybe even a little later," Warner says. "My wife was cooking dinner, I remember. And I looked through the glasses and saw the Norbois kid talking to these guys."

"What else did they talk about at the bar that night?" Hugh asks. "You say it was about two weeks ago you overheard this?"

Warner thinks. "It was right after the bodies were found. Maybe the next evening . . . ?"

"The bodies were found two weeks ago yesterday," Hugh says. "On July 22."

"It was the night of the twenty-third I heard them," Warner says. "They were both feeling no pain. They said something about how that asshole thought he could tell people what was what, did he think he owned the fucking lake? That kind of talk."

"But nothing more about the killings."

"Just that they mentioned how big the house looked from the outside. As if they'd been inside. At least, that's what came to my mind. I don't know, maybe it doesn't sound like much—"

"I'm glad you told me," Hugh says. "Anything else you remember?" Warner shakes his head, and Hugh says, "I'd like you to stop by the office and make a statement, if you would."

Warner sighs. "I thought you might. You going to talk to them about it? Listen, I'm not the nervous type. But it might be better if you just said somebody overheard them. I mean the place was packed that night."

"I won't say who told me." He concentrates his attention on Warner, facing away from the windows, away from the view. It's worth a million times what the house costs. *Talk about owning the lake.*

"Thanks." Warner looks at his watch. "I'm in kind of a rush today. But I'll be back up on Thursday."

"That's fine. Mind if I take this calendar along with me?"

"Yeah, no problem. I'll get it back, right?"

"Sure." He wouldn't be a bit surprised if Warner had a drawer full of them.

"I didn't really know the Norbois family," Warner says, as he walks Hugh to the door. "I talked to them a few times on the beach, that's about all. They kept pretty much to themselves. But then, so do we. You don't come up here to socialize. You come to get away from all that. The paper says there were no living relatives. That true?"

"No," says Hugh. "There's a few. They live out of state."

"Well, it's a gorgeous piece of property. Too bad it's got such a history now. I mean, who'd want to buy it?"

Given the way property values are climbing, some developer will undoubtedly snatch this piece up the minute it's on the market. The killings would be a good gimmick: *Safest property on the shoreline; lightning never strikes twice.*

Warner shakes Hugh's hand. "Yeah, your dad and I sure had some good times on that Michigan team. We mowed 'em down that year."

"Yes, sir." Hugh climbs into the patrol car. As

he leaves he can almost hear Warner's terse, "Go, Blue!" cut through the air behind him.

The one-story frame cottages sit, side by side, on two small lots that share a driveway. Two signs are nailed to a small maple: DIBOLD / POTTS.

The property—mostly hardwoods with a few scattered hemlocks—is shaded and well kept. An empty boat trailer is parked between the two lots, beside a silver Airstream.

"Do something for you?" a voice calls out as he approaches.

"Hope so," he returns pleasantly, spotting the man near the driveway. "I'm looking for Joe Dibold."

"That's me." The heavyset man is wearing swim trunks and a white T-shirt. Hugh introduces himself.

"Wondered when you'd be getting around to us," the man says. "This about the murders on the bluff?"

Hugh nods. "Just talking with people up and down the beach. Seeing if they heard anything that night."

The door to the other cottage opens and Dibold gives a wave. "Hey, Ray. Sheriff wants to have a word."

A bald man with an egg-shaped torso shambles over. "Ray Potts. Glad t'meetcha." He extends a meaty hand.

"You guys lived here a long time?"

"My dad bought the place in '72," Ray Potts says. "Sold the lot next door to this guy's folks"—he indicates Dibold—"a few years back."

"How long you been up this year?"

"Since mid-June," Dibold says. "Plant closed down for retooling. Supposed to be for two weeks, but then they laid everybody off. Production was down."

"They're talkin' about calling us back maybe next month," says Potts. "Longest layoff since '93."

"You guys have any acquaintance with the Norbois family?"

They both shake their heads. Dibold says, "They had a boat down at the dock, a Day Sailor. I seen 'em out in it a few times, that's about all."

"Never talked to them?"

"Maybe once or twice. To say 'hi.'"

"Didn't have a run-in with one of the sons about six weeks ago?"

"Run-in?" Potts's voice scales upward, a bit too innocently.

Dibold's head jerks. "Wait a minute. Yeah," he says. "That kid. Remember, Ray? When we were haulin' that hunk of driftwood? He was kinda pissed off at us."

"*That guy?* Was he one of the ones got killed?"

"I wouldn't call it a run-in exactly," Dibold says. "We was just—"

"Remember what day it was?" Hugh cuts him off. May as well keep them scurrying.

"Yeah, the twenty-fifth," Dibold says. "June twenty-fifth, I remember exactly 'cause we were leaving the next day for the Soo to do some fishing."

"And then we heard later there's some law about movin' stuff when it's in the water. Only thing is, that old derelict was down in front of our place for years."

"Yeah, we were wonderin' when that law was even passed," says Potts.

"About thirty years ago," Hugh says. "I heard you guys were talking one night up at the Outback. Thought you might've seen something or heard something."

The two do not look at each other. Dibold shakes his head.

"What I remember about that day was that it was damn hot. And we had words with that kid."

"That shipwreck disappeared from our place about four or five years ago," Potts says. "We thought they could've even been the ones who moved it."

"I don't remember hearing any gunshots or anything even like that," Potts says firmly.

"Yeah, we're pretty far away," Dibold agrees. "Sound doesn't carry all that well. With the bluffs and all."

"You guys own any guns?" Hugh asks.

Silence. Potts, scratching at a flaming patch of skin on his upper arm, says, "I don't think mine's here right now."

"We got rifles," Dibold says. "We use 'em for hunting mostly. In the fall."

"No shooting rats at the dump, huh?"

"Nah, never."

Yeah, I'll bet. Aloud Hugh says, "Well, thanks for your time . . . Oh, yeah. Ever been inside the Norbois place?"

"Who, us?" They both shake their heads. "No way."

"We don't get invited up there much," Potts says.

"Well, thanks," says Hugh. "Appreciate it."

"Probably some people been up there," Dibold says. "You know, looking things over. It bein' a crime scene and all."

Potts isn't interested in pursuing this. He is scratching furiously now. "So, what's the fine for movin' a shipwreck?" Opting for the lesser crime, if there's a choice.

"Not sure," Hugh says. "Call the DNR, they can tell you. Looks like you got into some poison ivy there."

A gloomy nod. "Cleaning out my woodpile. Oughta know by now what the stuff looks like."

"Bad year." Hugh nods in sympathy. "You guys take care now."

He walks away slowly; slow enough to rattle them, he hopes. *Yahoos.* He wishes they didn't make it quite so easy to look down on them. He also wishes it didn't give him this much pleasure, seeing them squirm.

One thing is certain, though: all three men— Warner, Potts, and Dibold—agree that Stephen Norbois was alive and well at 6 P.M. on the evening of June 25. And if he believes his wife, Valerie, there's no way Roger Frisch could have done those murders and been home in bed by nine o'clock that same night.

HIDING IN PLAIN SIGHT

CONGRATULATIONS," Mack Gellar says, his voice crackling over the cell phone from Grayling. "Gives you faith in the system. At least we got one of these crimes off the books."

"I think maybe we just hounded him to death," Hugh says. "I don't think he did it, Mack. One of the victims was seen on the beach at six o'clock. By three witnesses. According to his wife, Frisch was home in bed by nine o'clock on the night of the murder."

"According to his wife." Mack drops it like a

stone. "I dunno. Could be she has some interest in protecting his name?"

"I believe her, Mack."

"You do."

Hugh sighs. "The perp is dead. Long live the perp. Look, the guy who did this also took time out from his busy schedule to rape both female victims."

"You saying because he's an embezzler, he can't be a rapist?"

"I'm saying he doesn't have time to be a rapist. I'm saying if he's an embezzler, doing away with six people is overkill."

"What's all this resistance about, anyway, Hugh? Suppose he's just not that smart? Suppose he's a nutball? And he's suddenly got a big problem on his hands and this is the only way he knows to solve it. I vote for what it looks like. You guys start moving in and Frisch feels the heat. He decides to check out before you get a chance to set the hook. He's a depressive, you said. Who knows how they operate?"

"I'm a depressive," Hugh says. "I know. We're not that organized. This thing was well planned. And it was an ambush. It's the only way it'd ever work."

"Frisch was broke and about to be fired, maybe sent to jail. He was trying to figure out some way—any way—to keep that from happening. He was an embezzler, and they had him dead to rights. I think you're reaching."

"Yep, they sure did. And it was no secret. And soon the entire office staff would know it, thanks to Anne Ransome."

"So?"

"So, what did he have to gain by killing them?" He glances out of his window, studying the asphalt road, with its heat waves rolling up like a shimmering curtain. He was hoping for some support here; instead it's more of the same.

"Maybe he hired somebody to do it," Mack says at last.

"A hired killer who's a rapist on the side," Hugh says. "Now who's reaching?"

"Okay, so who are you pushing? Not that loopy caretaker and his brother, I hope."

"No. They haven't got the organizational skills."

"Not to mention the fact that ballistics came back negative on their guns," Mack says, his tone taking on the enforced patience of a man whose valuable time is being wasted. "Looks pretty open and shut to me. And it doesn't make a whole lot of sense, wasting the county's time and money on something that's as good as solved."

"Yeah, okay, I hear you."

For a moment he is reminded of his days at Police Academy, when he and Mack and Kevin would argue extremes of investigation versus fiscal responsibility by the hour. Usually it was Mack the Practical against him and Kevin.

"Kevin's the one with the real problem," Mack says. "He can't stand it that his guy is still out there, planning who knows what, while he sits waiting for the next shoe to drop. It's a bitch."

And this one isn't? Distancing is what makes it easier for the ones who have to clean up the mess. But distancing isn't going to help him solve this crime; nor will it answer his doubts. *A nutball.* Give it a name and let it rest. Except there has to be a better reason for these killings. Who was the catalyst, the primary victim, if it wasn't Edward Norbois? Did he or she see it coming?

The article he tore out of the *Free Press* lies, unfolded, on the seat beside him. He's read it through twice, can almost recite it by heart:

At 5:30 on the Sunday morning of
June 12, two cars pulled away from
a million-dollar gray stucco house
on Tilbury Way in the posh suburb
of Ann Arbor Estates.

In the two cars were a "model"
family: Edward Norbois, wealthy
publisher and advertising executive;
his attractive wife, Paige, and their

four children: Derek, 19, Stephen,
17, David, 13, and Nicole, 10.

The Norbois family was bound
for their Lake Michigan cottage in
the Blessed area, north of Petoskey.
Nobody in Ann Arbor would ever
see the family again.

Less than two weeks later, all six
were dead—victims of a mass murderer . . .

On the back of the page is the article about the
serial killings. Camilla Reusse's photograph leaps
out at him, as it did the first time he read it. The
high cheekbones and slanted, oriental-looking eyes.
The nose that reminds him of Egyptian aristocracy.
*Why are there no sketches of her among these piles
of pictures?*

Camilla Reusse disappeared the evening of
March 15. Her body was found April 29. *Six
weeks.* What was Derek Norbois thinking about
all the time the search for this girl went on? Did
he have some idea of what happened to her? Is
that why there are no sketches of her?

A third-year art school student from Saline . . .
working part-time for a local stockbroker . . . disappeared after leaving a beer party in Delhi Park.
Wasn't one of the other victims an art student?

He stops the car, pulls over to the side of the

road. Picking up the article, he quickly skims the other bios. Here it is: Jane Peterson, the second victim. *An art student at Eastern Michigan in Ypsilanti* . . .

Is it possible Derek knew this girl also? Both of them being in art school seems coincidental. But then again, maybe not. He doesn't remember a sketch resembling this second coed in Derek's collection either.

Why the obsession with this? *You tend to get bogged down in useless detail, DeWitt.* He can hear Kevin's voice, lecturing him from fifteen years ago at the academy.

He starts the car, pulls back onto the highway. In less than ten minutes he has arrived at the Norbois cabin. The caution tape is starting to show signs of wear. Time to take it down. He gets out of the patrol car, opens the trunk, and grabs one of the masks, slipping it into place as he approaches the cabin. The watch has been called off; nothing to protect here anymore.

He climbs the stairway to the bedroom area and enters the older boys' room. There are Derek's sketches, lying strewn across one of the twin beds. No sketches of Camilla Reusse among them. None of Jane Peterson, either. Everything is as it was the last time he was here. Black blood-stains on the floor. They have soaked permanently into the wood now. Dime-sized spatters of dried blood across the blankets. He turns away, oddly disappointed. He was so sure of finding something here. *What, for God's sake?* And if he did find something, what would it prove? So what if Derek happened to know Jane Peterson? How is that going to get him any closer to finding Derek's killer?

He sits on the edge of the bed opposite the sketches and again fishes the article out of his wallet. *"Camilla Reusse . . . a third-year art student . . . working part-time for a local stockbroker . . ."*

James Faber is a stockbroker. James Faber knew Paige Norbois. Could he have also known Camilla Reusse? *A long shot,* he thinks, dialing police headquarters in Ann Arbor. *About the longest shot ever.* He asks to speak to the clerk in Records.

"Take a look through the files on Camilla Reusse," he says, "and see if a James Faber was ever questioned in connection with her disappearance."

"Sure. Want to hang on while I check?"

"No. I'll call you back."

"Give me ten minutes or so."

He goes outside to wait in the patrol car. The cabin gives him the creeps. Its massive, ominous presence makes the woods surrounding it seem insignificant, almost an afterthought. He wonders if, in building it, Edward Norbois's intention was to establish an instant heritage. Like Jack London's mansion in the Valley of the Moon. Wolf House, he called it. He remembers as a kid, going to visit the valley with his folks and coming upon that disturbing, half-destroyed mansion rotting away in the California woods. With its broken beams overgrown with moss, its foundation about to sink into the floor of the forest, it still had the power to draw darkness to it.

He glances at his watch; dials the phone.

"Okay, here's what I got. James Faber came in on March 18 to give a statement. Camilla Reusse worked for him from September until the time of her disappearance. She was at the office until five-thirty on the afternoon of March 15, after which she left, and that was the last time he saw her."

"Thanks," he says. "Thanks very much for your trouble."

He hangs up and sits in the patrol car, staring out through the windshield at the tight huddle of blue spruce trees bordering the driveway. They've been there a lot longer than four years. Some of the newer plantings are too close, also. Because people always want instant privacy. But these have grown up on the property and will eventually spread their branches and snare each other in an unhealthy embrace. *Nature sometimes makes mistakes, too.*

Hugh dials another number.

"Hey, my man," Billy Shaw says. "Just about to give you a call. So far no match with Frisch on anything we found. VNTRs look totally different. Doesn't mean he's home free, but I'd say it's unlikely he's your rapist."

"Either way, I'd say he's home free," Hugh says.

Billy laughs. "You're a dark one, DeWitt. We haven't gotten far enough to tell anything much about the other samples yet. The ones of the LaChappelle boys."

"That's okay," Hugh says. "There's another favor I need from you, Billy. I'd like you to check out something else for me."

ANALYSIS AND DELAY

T HE EMMET COUNTY Medical Clinic is closed for the day when Hugh drives up. He parks, waves at Angela through the window of Coffee Talk as he knocks on the door. Doc DeVere answers with a sheaf of papers in his hand.

"Got 'em all ready," he says. "Just finishing up here." He hands Hugh the Certificates of Death, neatly typed, signed with his confident scrawl.

Hugh glances at the top form, done in triplicate: blue, pink, yellow. *Manner of Death:* trau-

matic injury. *Cause of Death:* cranial bullet
wound. It is Derek Norbois's certificate.

He flips to Edward Norbois: *Cause of Death:*
cardiac arrest due to severed aorta. So Edward is
the only one who certainly was dead before the
bullet entered his brain. What does this say about
the others?

"GSR on the wife and youngest boy. Looks like
they were shot from up close," Doc says.

"How about the others? Any gunshot residue
at all?"

"Hardly a trace. The little girl was killed by
multiple blows to the head with a blunt object.
Probably a hammer."

Why did Faber think he had to kill the whole
family? Surely he could have found some way to
get Paige alone. Is it that he thought he'd be a less
likely suspect if all of them were killed? But then,
why the rapes? Why rape Nicole?

"I'm sending these off tomorrow," Doc says. "I
need to get those cousins off my back. I've had
half a dozen calls from that woman with the
Spanish name. 'Can't you people understand that
we need to settle this estate? We need those death
certificates, blah, blah, blah.' Like I'm supposed to
sweat her adding to her millions. Is it true they'll
own everything, including that cabin?"

"Looks like it," Hugh says. "But I wouldn't worry.
I don't think they're planning to move up here."

"I heard ballistics came back negative on the LaChappelles' guns."

"Jesus, this town gets smaller and smaller. Where'd you hear that? No, never mind."

Doc is insulted. "What am I, some guy who parks his sailboat down at the marina? I've got a right to know this stuff, don't I?"

"Sorry," Hugh says. "I'm getting testy. Too many reporters. Too much bad information out there."

"Bad information?"

"More like no information. Nothing good to go on. And what there is points to the wrong people."

"This has got to be one helluva strain, Hugh," Doc says. "You been sleeping okay? Can I do something for you?"

"I'm fine. I just . . . I've got other things on my mind, that's all."

"Like what?"

"Just . . . Karen's been on me. She thinks I ought to get a physical." *Shit.* He had absolutely no thought of going there today. He'd better get out of here before things get dicey.

"Karen's right." Doc jumps on it. "How long has it been? Five years? I bet I haven't checked you over since the fire up at Banfield's. I know for sure you haven't been in to see me since Petey died."

At this, Hugh's body goes stiff, and he feels an urgent need for a deep breath; he reaches for it, but no luck. He concentrates on rolling the sheaf of certificates into a tight cylinder.

"That's a big event for someone to absorb," Doc says gently. "You need to start paying attention to your body, Hugh. I know the way you just keep on keepin' on. You're like your daddy."

"It isn't that," he says, still searching for air. "It's not about that, Martin, that was three years ago, my God." In any case, he doesn't want to discuss it, not now, not in the company of the man who signed his son's death certificate. "It's just this damned case. The stupid waste of it all. That little girl."

"Yeah. It's a shitty thing, all right." Doc takes the papers away from him. "Here, you're getting those all wrinkled. So, what are your symptoms?"

"Nothing, really," he says. "Nothing serious."

"If you don't tell me, Mr. Stoic, I'm calling Karen. You know I'll do it, too. Your health is not something we're gonna fool with here."

Stoyk. He pronounces it in one syllable. Hugh has to smile.

"Listen, if it's heart stuff—"

"It's not heart stuff."

"Because with your history—"

"Martin. It's not my heart. I can't get it up. That's all. It's nothing."

A silence. Then: "Jesus, don't you ever watch TV? They got a cure for that now. Pop a pill and rise at will. How long has this been going on?"

He knows exactly how long, but he's not about to say it out loud, refuses to discuss this topic without any goddamned preparation. "So, if that's the case you can just write a prescription and that'll take care of it, right?"

"Not so fast," Doc says. "After the physical." He flips through his calendar. "I got some time next Tuesday."

"I don't know . . ."

"Yeah, you do. One o'clock. Write it down. Bring a urine specimen. You got any idea what might be causing it?"

Hugh shakes his head, moving quickly toward the door. *Get out, get some air, that's the ticket.*

"Because I got a theory. That is, if you're interested."

"I can wait," Hugh says, opening it and hustling out, moving past Coffee Talk without a glance inside; he doesn't want to catch Angela peering at him through the window, doesn't want to read something into that.

"Well, you were right on the money." Billy Shaw leads him into the lab where five young men sit, crouched in their separate cubicles, hovering over an array of instruments. *Where are all the women?* Hugh wonders.

"The key was mitochondrial DNA. One of the sites of variation. Here, take a look. I set this up just for you." He seats Hugh at an empty microscope.

"See that little package outside the nucleus? That's your ticket right there."

"What am I supposed to be looking at?"

"See how those two lines are identical? You can read snippets of unique variable sequence mitochondrial DNA and trace maternal lineage."

"Billy, I don't care who the mother was."

"Get a clue, DeWitt," Billy says. "This is the stuff that only the female passes on. Nobody's is the same, nobody's in the entire world. What I'm saying is the guy who raped the coeds has the same mother as the guy who raped both Paige and Nicole Norbois. So unless he's got a sibling out there and they're taking turns, we got us a match."

Bingo. He knew it. There were too many similarities—the viciousness, the rapes, the elaborate steps taken to hide the bodies. The longer, the better. Did this guy read the newspapers every day, checking to see if the stupid cops had come up with a clue? Did he revisit the bodies in order to relive the moment? To savor the kill?

"You think one of these samples that we're still working on might be the killer?" Billy asks.

"Maybe," Hugh says. "How're you coming on the James Faber sample?"

"It doesn't strike you as odd that he gave it up without a whimper?"

"They all did, Billy. Look, Faber was having an affair with her. And, as it happens, one of the dead coeds worked for him."

"Oh, Hercule," says Billy. "I think you got yourself a perp. Well, don't forget where you heard it. When I write up my proposal for a probe that reads three billion letters at a crack."

"I won't."

"Helluva lot better than hiring a psychic to smell somebody's underpanties, isn't it?"

"You're a sick guy, Billy."

"Yeah. I think it might've cost me my last marriage."

———

The psychic has definitely taken up residence in Ann Arbor—examining various articles of clothing, visiting the murder sites, interviewing relatives of the dead girls. He's even holding his own news conferences.

Hugh pulls into the parking lot of the station house, wondering how Ann Arbor Police Chief Kevin Watkins's ulcer is doing these days.

"What's so important it couldn't wait until

tomorrow?" he asks as he escorts Hugh into his office.

"I've just been to see Billy." He tells Kevin the news.

"Jesus, I don't believe it," Kevin says. "So what we know for sure is, the guy who raped your two is the same guy who raped all of mine."

"That's what we know. I'm thinking we need to keep a good eye on James Faber. He's the guy I like the best."

"I know we talked to him after the Reusse girl's disappearance. But, Hughie, we questioned a zillion people. And we've got crossovers everywhere. Hell, I've got guys on the list who knew all four of those women!"

"But nobody else who knew the Norbois family, I'm betting."

"How long before Billy's got something definitive with the DNA?"

"Could be another couple of weeks. This stuff takes time."

"Yeah, what we don't have. I'm holding my breath there's not another one in the works. It's been five weeks since the Levin murder. He must be getting antsy."

"Unless he's getting scared," Hugh says. "That's a possibility."

"Jesus, whatever gave him the balls to hand over that sample voluntarily?" Kevin shakes his head. "Okay, we keep this under wraps until we hear from Billy. What about the gun? Faber probably owns one, huh? After Nine-Eleven everybody in town's gotten gun-happy. We're processing registrations at three times the rate we did before. You're not going to tell the Widow Frisch any of this, are you?"

"No, of course not."

"Yeah. It's best to leave old Roj as the prime suspect until we get things wrapped up." Kevin sighs. "It'd sure be nice, wouldn't it? If we nailed him and he did us this huge favor and confessed?"

Walking out of police headquarters, Hugh marvels at Kevin's equanimity over all of this, now that their two cases have suddenly become one. Would he have been this calm, this philosophical, if the situations were reversed? Kevin has been working on the serial killings nonstop for over a year. If the Norbois murders are solved in less than a month, how will it play out in the headlines? *There's never been a case like this,* he thinks. *None of the old rules apply. And it isn't over yet.*

His cell phone rings as he gets into the patrol car: it is Gina Keyes.

"I thought of something else," she says. "Something Derek said after Camilla Reusse was . . . after she died. He told me he had a bad feeling about it. At first I thought he just meant her being killed and all . . . how awful it was. But now I really think he knew something. Only when I tried to get him to tell me, he just closed up. He had a way of stopping you cold. You just knew you wouldn't get anywhere, no matter how hard you pushed."

"I've got a question for you, Gina," Hugh says. "About Maura James's uncle. Did you ever happen to meet him?"

"Once. When he came to visit her at the house."

"Do you remember his name, by any chance?"

"No," she says. A pause at the other end. "But don't you know who he is? I saw you with him. You were talking to him the other day. At the funeral."

CROSSED PURPOSES

Maura's lights are still on when Hugh arrives, although it is after eleven o'clock at night. He parks the patrol car in the alley behind her house. He doesn't want the neighbors getting nervous. As he climbs the stairs to her apartment he hears her door open above him.

"Sheriff DeWitt. Just in time for pizza."

He makes it to the third-floor landing only slightly out of breath.

"How old are you?" she asks abruptly.

"I'm thirty-eight. Why?"

She steps aside to let him in. "I was just thinking. You're almost the same age as my daddy. But you seem a lot younger."

"I don't feel so young these days," he says.

"Responsibilities, huh?"

"You got it."

"They'll kill you if you let them. Like this house. I've thought about selling it so many times. It's a lot of work—taking care of it, keeping it rented. On the other hand, it's a cash cow."

"Is it?"

"Oh, for sure. I don't do anything to it, and it's almost always full. Plus, I don't even have to own a car. I can get wherever I need to in this town on my bike."

"I admire you," Hugh says. "You're a modern-day pioneer."

She gives him a look. "And this is what you came up here to tell me."

"Not exactly, no."

"What, then? At this hour of the night?"

"I need to borrow your gun, Maura."

She laughs. "Why? What's up?"

"I want to run some tests on it."

"What kind of tests?"

"Ballistics."

"Uh-oh." She shakes her head. "I promise you it hasn't even been fired in the last three years."

"Is that how long you've owned it?"

"I don't own it exactly."

"That's right. What did you say—your uncle gave it to you? Was it a loan?"

"Sort of."

"You know, I'm thinking I might know this uncle of yours. What's his name?"

She looks back at him, her face expressionless. "James Faber."

"Ah, yes. James Faber. Why didn't you tell me that before?"

"You didn't ask."

"Like I didn't ask you if you knew about this uncle having an affair with Derek's mother?"

A long silence. "I didn't know about it. Not until after Derek died."

"And who told you?"

"My mother. I heard about it from her. Anyway, what does that have to do with anything?" She's angry with him now, her anger covering up some other emotion; he's sure it's fear.

"Did you also know that your uncle knew Camilla Reusse? That she worked for him? And that he was questioned by the police after her disappearance?"

"Lots of people knew her. Lots of people knew all of those women. The police came here and questioned everybody on the block. So what?"

"Was Camilla Reusse having an affair with your uncle, too?"

"No! Listen, you don't even know him, he's a good man! He's not . . . he's had a very sad life. His only son died of leukemia . . ."

"Maura, did you introduce Derek to your uncle?"

"No."

"But your uncle knew who Derek was, didn't he? He knew he was living in your house. Did Derek know about the affair?"

"I haven't a fucking clue," she snaps. "What if he did? What does that prove?" She looks away, toward the windows. Her shoulders lift slightly. "My uncle hasn't done anything wrong."

"You want to help him prove that?"

"How?"

"Give me the gun."

Her eyes narrow and she turns away from him. "The gun hasn't been out of my house. Not since the last time I took it to the bank. And then I returned it to the drawer. I told you it hasn't been fired in three years."

"You don't think it's possible someone could have stolen it?"

"Stolen it and then put it back again? No, I don't. I would have noticed."

"If that's so, then what are you worried about?"

"I'm not worried." She goes to the drawer and opens it, shoving the dishtowels around. "I don't have to give it to you," she says. "If you had a warrant, you'd have shown it to me."

"Right. It's strictly voluntary."

"Collecting guns all up and down the street, are you?"

He smiles, realizing suddenly why it is that he likes her so much; it is her courage. She spits in the face of danger. Just like his mother used to do. Witty, smart, honest. He wishes he didn't have to lie to her this way; he hopes to hell she isn't lying to him.

———

He walks out to the alley, the gun in his pocket, thinking back over their conversation. *Lots of people knew all of those women.* And she's right. He has looked up the first coed's address: Valerie Dennis. She lived only blocks away. And the second—Jane Peterson—was abducted somewhere between Hazlitt's restaurant and her apartment on Merrill Street, which is less than a mile from here. *Was it Paige Norbois who knew something? Or was it Derek? And what did they know?*

He feels a nervous thrill run across the backs of his hands. He doesn't have much time. *Wrap it up. Before anyone else figures it out. Before another innocent person gets in the murderer's way and he has to kill again.*

BEGGARS AND
HORSES

WE'RE GOING TO be late." Karen is staring at
her watch as they cross the highway above Pellston.

"No, we're not. It's a little after twelve. We'll
be right on time."

"Becky's cooked up a plan," Karen says, glancing out the window. "She wants us all to come
back to camp this November for an old-fashioned
Thanksgiving."

"What does that mean?" Hugh asks. "We exe-
cute our own turkey and eat corn pudding?"

"I don't know, but she's terribly excited about it."

"She gets excited about lots of things. Let's not get ourselves involved in something we really don't want to do."

"And how do we know we really don't want to do it?"

"We know we don't want to eat Thanksgiving dinner up in the dunes, don't we? What about your mom? Think she'd like that?"

"She'd love it. Admit it, Hugh. You're the one who doesn't want to do it." Again she looks away, toward the window. "Look! There's the new antique store Bev was talking about. She says their stuff is gorgeous. Not too pricey, either."

"New antiques," Hugh says. "How does that work, exactly?"

"Don't, Hugh."

"Don't what?"

"Just stop it. You've been arguing with everything I've said since you got up."

"*I've* been arguing?" He waits a moment, says cautiously, "Is this about me not wanting to move furniture this morning?"

She is staring steadfastly out the window. "Just tell me if you're going to act like this when we get there."

"Like what?"

"Because if you are, I'll just march right down to the lake and jump in and she can be humiliated by both parents at the same time."

"Look, I'm sorry about the moving experiment," he says. "I just wasn't in the mood."

"And don't call it an *experiment!* You *demean* everything!"

He waits a moment; tries again. "Karey, whatever it is that's bugging you, I swear I'm not doing it on purpose."

"I guess that's supposed to make me feel better."

Okay, end of effort. Feeling injured and illused, he keeps his eyes on the road, turns his attention to his own thoughts. And, against his will, there's Becky—not as the ten-year-old he knows and loves but as the teenager she'll soon become—complete with stiletto heels, hair dyed blue and cut like handfuls of hay, the triple-pierced ears, the skintight skirt and top barely covering her body. And some scruffy jerk from Levering comes to their door to ride her away on his Triumph. Someone he's already had to arrest for drunken driving.

Where do they come from, these thoughts? But he knows their source: Maura. A drunk for a father. An uncle soon to be arrested for the most heinous of crimes. She's had no guidance; what are her chances? Underneath all that makeup and bizarre attire is a beautiful young woman. No doubt, a beautiful child. *Like Becky. Like Nicole. The world is a stinking place.* It's one hundred degrees outside. The damning brilliance of the sun on the fields makes them look crushed and defeated.

"Whatever in the world are you thinking?" asks Karen.

He shakes his head. "Don't ask."

She slides closer to him. "Sorry," she says.

"Me, too." He gives her arm a squeeze. "You're right, Karey. I'm in a lousy mood these days."

"When this is all over, you and Kevin need to go on a long fishing trip. Maybe to Canada."

"If he's still speaking to me."

"Why wouldn't he be?"

"I don't know."

"You're sure it's Faber, aren't you?"

"I've got no proof. I'm waiting for some word from Billy."

"But the *gun*. If the shell casings match—"

"*If* they match. We have to make certain everything's locked up tight before we make a move."

"And in the meantime . . ."

"Right. In the meantime. That's what's making me so fucking nervous."

"Does Kevin want to arrest him now?"

"We keep switching positions. Neither of us wants to screw this up. If we arrest him too soon, we run the risk of having some hotshot lawyer nail us in court for jumping the gun."

"Did it have something to do with the affair, Hugh? Is that why he killed her?"

"I don't know. What I think is she knew something. Or was about to figure out something. Maybe she and Derek were figuring it out together. And Faber realized he couldn't let them live, knowing what they knew."

"I can't get used to this; that the same person who murdered that whole family killed all those girls—it's truly awful," she says. "How can one person be so evil?"

Evil is rampant, he thinks. Resolutely he pushes the thought aside. He's going to watch his daughter perform in a gymkhana at a horse farm this afternoon. He's supposed to be having fun. He'll do it if it kills him.

———

They *are* late, and Becky is waiting for them in the parking lot, wearing her jodhpurs and plaid shirt, pacing frantically. As soon as they pull up she turns and runs away at a fast clip toward the horse barns. They hurry to the bleachers, set up around a large dirt ring. The dust is heavy in the air; the stands are full of people who have arrived on time and are patiently awaiting the show.

"There are the Wolds," Karen says, pointing

to the far end. Hugh is in no hurry. As soon as they are seated he will be compelled to watch his daughter doing the risky and dangerous things that, up until now, he has only had to imagine.

Fourth in a long line of nervous performers, she clutches the reins of a wild-eyed animal who looks as huge to him as a goddamned elephant, even from this distance. He tries to seem like the experienced father of a veteran camper, but inwardly he's terrified.

The Wolds are the perfect spectators—thrilled with every performance, greeting each new rider with cheers and waves, and every few minutes shouting, *"Is this amazing, or what?"*

Becky's turn comes all too soon for Hugh. As she rounds their end of the ring, the toe of her boot suddenly slips the stirrup and she falls forward over the horse's neck. His heart plunges. *She's hurt, she's falling . . . !* But no. In an instant she rights herself, regains her footing, and moves the big bay smoothly through the rest of his paces. The crowd loves it. They stamp their feet and cheer. Hugh realizes he has seized Karen's hand in a grip of iron. Shamed, he lets go.

"She's a tough one!" Ed Wold elbows him happily. "Takes after her old man!"

"Isn't she just a *natural?*" Karen whispers in his ear. Why she would want to see this as a positive is anyone's guess; it only proves their daughter will insist on continuing these dangerous acts, going to riskier and riskier heights. He squeezes Karen's elbow tightly against his ribs, keeping his mouth shut for once.

———

"So, what did you think, Daddy?" Forehead shining, damp hair plastered against her cheeks, Becky leans down from her horse's neck to give him a sweaty hug.

"I thought you were great, Beck," he says.

"Isn't Duke a sweetheart? He's the best horse in the stable. He's the highest jumper, and I get to ride him every day."

Oh, great. Hugh smiles back at her, determined to catch the wave of her enthusiasm. She introduces them to the owners, the groomers, the wranglers and handlers; even the cooks and kitchen help.

"Can Jenny and Donna spend the night, Mom?" she asks.

"I think we've had enough togetherness for a while," Ed Wold says. "Jenny needs to come home tonight."

The rest of the parents agree. Hugh gives his daughter a hand with her duffel. "You can all get together tomorrow."

The cars begin the parade down the dusty two-track. Becky yawns in spite of herself. "I took tons of pictures," she says. "Can we get them developed right away? I don't see why we couldn't all stay together, just for one more night."

"We've been missing you," Karen says. "Let's just have family night together. We'll have fun, I promise."

"I've got something I have to do," Hugh says. "But it won't take long."

"That's okay," Karen says. "We'll go with you."

"No, I'll drop you off at home." And at her look: "It's just a couple of quick errands, I promise."

An ominous silence. Becky leans forward over the front seat. "Are you two guys fighting again?"

Something hasn't felt right to him ever since the last time he was here. He climbs the steps to the bedrooms of the Norbois cabin. There they are—the half-packed suitcases, with their stuff spilling out across the beds. *Why spilling out? They were packing, weren't they, not unpacking?*

The blood spatters in the boys' room, on the closet wall, a series of elongated drops, indicating issuance from exit wounds. The pile of sketches scattered across the bed, as if someone had been studying them. Why? Why would Derek be doing this in the midst of packing for a trip? *And if it wasn't Derek. Or Stephen. If it was the killer, what was he looking for?*

Hugh glances up at the wall opposite the closet, next to the two beds. Several other framed drawings are hanging there. More of Derek's work. The first is the shoreline immediately below Route 119; Hugh recognizes it at once. He walks over to lift it from the wall, turns it over in his hands. It looks professionally framed. Stiff brown paper stretched tight, fastened to the frame with brads and glue.

Another drawing hangs beside this one: the Norbois cabin, viewed from the sloping hill behind it. This sketch is larger than the first, done in pen and ink with a faint wash of color. The back door of the cabin is open, catching the light so as to reflect an image of a canoe lying in the grass. A few feet away is the actual canoe, upside down, with its stern wedged against a rock.

He remembers this exact scene from the day he and Ian discovered the bodies. Except the door wasn't open; it was closed tight. *Everything locked up.* He studies the sketch a moment, then lifts it from the wall. The framing looks amateurish, sloppy. The wooden rectangle is backed with a piece of shirt cardboard and fastened with cheap metal triangles shoved at odd intervals into the edges.

Hugh sits down on the bed, still holding the picture in his hands. He picks gently at the triangles; they slide out easily under his fingernail. He loosens and lifts the cardboard from its resting place inside the frame.

And there it is: staring up at him. A drawing of a girl, a brunette, sitting at a picnic bench. Her back is to the table; her left arm is lifted, resting against the top. Her finely chiseled features—the straight Egyptian nose and faintly oriental-looking cheekbones—look exactly like the newspaper clipping. Her other hand rests on the knee of the person sitting next to her.

Hugh feels his heart banging against his ribs. This, then, is what Derek Norbois knew. And only Derek knew it. Derek and the two people in the picture. *But why did you wait on this? Who did you think you were protecting? You must have had some reason, but what was it? Misguided loyalty? Love? Or were you simply overconfident? Sure you could handle this without involving anyone else in it, without telling anyone what you knew. Or were you truly afraid? Afraid to accept what you knew it must mean?*

Did you believe you could still be wrong? You were worried enough to hide the evidence. What were you thinking? What were you waiting for? Whatever your reasons, Derek, they were what killed you.

MISSING PIECES

MACK GELLAR SAYS he'll have what you need in a couple of hours," Fredda assures him. "Will that be soon enough?"

"Yeah."

"Where are you?" she asks.

"Saginaw. I'll be in Ann Arbor by ten this morning."

"Good luck," she says.

He hangs up, feeling as if he's been on the phone for twelve hours straight. Not much of a family evening, he reflects. And this morning

Karen was up making his breakfast over his protests.

"You need to eat," she insisted. "Will you be back tonight?"

He promised to do his best. Now he picks up the phone once again to call Kevin.

"Everything's all set for us, buddy," Kevin says. "He's coming in today at eleven."

"Perfect. Mack will call you with the ballistics report."

"You think he's going to give it up?" Kevin asks.

"Not a chance. I'm betting he's not going to admit to a fucking thing."

"Yeah, that's my guess. Hey, as soon as this is wrapped up what say we go fishing in Manitoba?"

"Karen thinks what I need are a few sessions with a good psychiatrist."

Kevin laughs. "Glad she didn't include me. And don't you go suggesting it to Delia either."

———

He arrives at police headquarters in Ann Arbor at ten o'clock on the dot. A few minutes later, Guy Mason's Honda rolls into the parking lot.

"I got your message," he says. "About Maura. What's up?"

"I'll tell you when we get inside."

Together they walk down the hallway toward Kevin's office.

"I came a little early," Guy says. "It's not every day you get to meet the chief of police."

"Remember that course you mentioned a while ago? The one you took about the deviant individual? Did they talk about profiling in there?"

"Sure."

"What'd they tell you?"

Guy thinks a minute. "About the only thing I remember is that people who do violent crimes are often in denial. Like if they never admit the crime to themselves, it's as though it never really happened."

"Interesting," Hugh says. "You didn't happen to run into your landlady this morning, did you?"

"No. She's probably still in bed." He grins. "She had a late night, I think. Why?"

"No reason." They have reached Kevin's office and Hugh opens the door. Kevin looks up from his desk.

"Hey. I've been waiting for you." *Smooth as butter.* He stretches his hand across the desk toward Guy. "This the one you wanted me to meet?"

"This is Guy Mason," Hugh says. "Guy, Chief Watkins."

Guy takes the hand, shakes it firmly.

"I hear you're interested in becoming a cop," Kevin says. "Sheriff DeWitt filled you in on what a horseshit job it is, right? Otherwise he'd be lying. Here, sit down. Did he mention anything to you about the James girl?"

"The James girl." Guy grins. "Makes her sound like she's part of Jesse's gang."

"I didn't," Hugh says, turning to Guy. "Did you know that she owned a gun?"

"Maura? Are you kidding me?"

"You never saw it, huh?" Kevin asks. "Small, foreign model . . . ?"

Guy shakes his head. "What's she doing with a gun, anyway? You don't think she had anything to do with the murders . . . ?"

"Which murders?" Hugh asks.

"The ones up in Blessed. Isn't that what we're talking about?"

"Right," Kevin says. "All we know is that the gun was a .32-caliber semiautomatic with hollow-point bullets. General rifling characteristics determined it was probably a European make. Problem was, the evidence bullets were so badly damaged it'd be tough to determine anything from them."

"But then I got lucky," Hugh said. "I found a casing. Buried in the dirt outside the house."

"How does that help?" Guy asks. "I don't know much about gun stuff."

"The killer did," Hugh says. "It was the only casing he dropped. He must have taken the others with him."

"So we borrowed the James girl's gun," Kevin says, "and we're running ballistics on it."

"If the GRCs and breech marks match," Hugh says, "we've got our murder weapon."

Silence. Then: "You think Maura is involved in all this? That's hard to believe."

"Not Maura. Somebody she knows. Possibly her uncle," Hugh says. "See, it was his gun. Do you remember whether Derek ever took Maura up to the cabin in Blessed?"

Guy laughs. "You mean, like, to meet the folks? No way."

"When's the last time you were up there?"

"I told you. Last February. When we went cross-country skiing. Listen, I'm still trying to figure it out about her uncle. Why would he do something like that?"

Kevin shrugs. "Why does anybody do stuff like that? Why did somebody murder four college girls . . . strangle and rape them and leave their bodies to rot? The world's full of crazy people. What more can I say?"

"I'm wondering about this uncle of hers," Hugh says. "If he could have known where the cabin was."

"Lots of people knew about it," Guy says. "It

wasn't any secret. Anybody could've known where it was."

"Yeah," Kevin says. "Here's one thing we figured out about this killer. He doesn't like women much. Both the mother and the little girl were raped."

Guy shakes his head. "That's sick . . ."

"Yeah, pretty sick. But we don't think it was a sex crime. That was an afterthought," Hugh says. "What we think is that the killer was after something else. The rapes were just icing on the cake."

Another silence. "You know I'm thinking," Guy says, "that anybody could have broken into Maura's apartment and taken her gun."

"Except that her apartment wasn't broken into," Hugh says.

"Yeah, it's gotta be somebody close to her," says Kevin. "Somebody who had a key. Or knew how to get one. Because he'd plan on putting the gun back before she noticed it was missing."

"So you're saying somebody stole it, went up to Blessed and did the murders, and then put it back."

"Exactly," Hugh says. He shifts position in his chair. "Here's another odd thing. I heard you were at a beer party up in Blessed over Memorial Day weekend."

Guy looks at him. "That's not possible. I worked that whole weekend. At the bike shop."

"Do you remember the day we went to the

Norbois house?" Hugh asks. "And I asked you about those sketches?"

"Sure."

Hugh reaches across Kevin's desk. He picks up a manila folder. "I was wondering why there weren't any drawings of Camilla Reusse. Since Derek seems to have known her so well."

"Not all that well," Guy says.

"Really? Gina Keyes told me they were good friends. They spent time together."

Guy shrugs his shoulders. "Maybe he just never got around to it."

"Well, it seemed odd to me. I couldn't get it out of my mind. I kept looking and looking. And then I finally found one," Hugh says. "And now what I'm wondering is, what does it mean?"

He flips the manila folder open to reveal the sketch. Guy studies it in silence. At last he looks up.

"This is a picture of me," he says. "With some girl."

"It's a picture of you," Hugh says, "with Camilla Reusse. Sitting on the picnic bench in Maura James's backyard."

"No, it's not," Guy says. "That's not her. That's some girl I don't even remember, probably just some bimbo Derek knew."

"Look again," says Kevin, his voice steely.

"I don't need to. *I don't know Camilla Reusse. I never even met her.*" He looks from Kevin to

Hugh, his eyes revealing something new, something akin to fury.

"Here's what I'm thinking," Kevin says. "You killed this girl. And when the cops questioned you, you made a mistake; you said you didn't know her. But Derek knew that was a lie. Because he had this sketch of the two of you that he'd done in the backyard."

"So, what happened after that?" Hugh asks. "Did you ask him for the sketch? And when he refused to give it to you, you figured it meant he knew you'd killed her? Did you make another mistake and tell him you'd lied to the police? Exactly how did that whole thing play out?"

"You don't know what the fuck you're talking about," Guy says calmly. "He was always drawing pictures of people. He was a genius, he could draw any face from memory. That's what he did here—he drew a picture of her and then he stuck me in it. Just for the hell of it."

"Why would he do that?"

"Because he wanted to get me in trouble with the cops! Because he's an asshole! How the hell do I know?"

"That must have made you mad," Kevin says. "When he wouldn't hand over the sketch. Is that why you killed the rest of them, then? To punish Derek for being an asshole?"

"Oh, I get it now," he says. "Both you guys'

asses are on the line for this, right? You could lose your fuckin' jobs. You gotta come up with somebody and damned fast. So you pick me. Well, this isn't gonna happen. I didn't do a damned thing!"

"You needed a weapon," Kevin says. "You couldn't strangle them, not the way you did the women. But luckily you knew just where you could get a gun."

"I never killed anybody," Guy says stolidly. "Derek Norbois was my friend. His dad was my friend. His mother fuckin' *loved* me!"

"Must have been frustrating," Hugh says. "Going through all those drawings—first, the ones at the cabin and then the ones at the house. You did a good job with me that day. I really bought how upset you were about being there for the first time since the murders." He smiles. "But Derek did a good job, too. He worked at hiding that sketch. You want me to tell you where I finally found it?"

"I want to call my mother," Guy says. "I want to talk to a lawyer. And if that bitch Maura says I knew she had a gun, she's a cocksucking liar. I dumped her and called her a whore and she's pissed at me."

"You wrote the book on deviant behavior," Hugh says. "You ought to know."

"Fuck you," Guy says. "You lying pimp sheriff from Hicksville, *fuck you!*"

"Here." Kevin pushes the telephone at him. "Call your mother."

———

The two friends walk together down the hall. Kevin has scheduled the news conference for two o'clock, to announce the arrest in both the Blessed case and the four coed murders.

"Why'd he come an hour early?" Kevin asks. "He almost spooked me."

"Overconfident."

"You and me," Kevin says, "we put on a damn fine dog and pony show."

"Yeah, we're the dynamic duo," Hugh says gloomily.

"What's the matter?"

"I lost it at the end. That crack about him writing the book on deviant behavior."

"Oh, Christ, give it a rest," Kevin says. "I liked how you slipped it in about the last time he'd been up to Blessed. Is he a compulsive liar or what? He lies about stupid things that don't even matter. Why didn't he tell us in the first place he knew the Reusse girl? It wouldn't have made him look any more guilty than a half dozen other guys we were talking to. How'd you find that out about Memorial Day weekend, anyway?"

"I talked to the Maillot kid last night. Just on a whim. I remembered Nicole's friend, Lizzy Trout, telling us one of the older boys had a friend up and they partied until four in the morning. Sure enough, Denny Maillot says he met Mason at a beer party that Saturday night. Says he was driving a green Honda motorcycle."

"He looks like such a goddamned college boy. Who'd think it? Ten murders before he's twenty-one. That's gotta be some kind of record."

"I'll lay you odds on something else," Hugh says. "He was the one Coby saw running through the woods on Fourth of July weekend. After he killed the Levin girl in Muskegon he must have thought he'd mosey over and see how things were going in Blessed. The fact that Coby didn't see a car should have clued me in sooner."

"So why did he lie about being up there over Memorial Day?" Kevin asks. "I don't get it."

"I think he felt guilty. I'm betting it was the weekend he made up his mind to do it. He was checking things out. Observing family habits. Making sure the front door was always unlocked. He knew they'd be leaving early the morning of the twenty-sixth, so they'd be getting ready the night before, and they'd all be there."

"You think he gets it that he's toast?"

"Nah. He'll be telling them in prison for twenty years how he got railroaded."

"Yeah, we hope," Kevin says. "Lucky for us we've got the murder weapon."

"Lucky for us he's so fucking arrogant."

"Let's face it, where he screwed up was not keeping his stories straight. Telling us he didn't know the Reusse girl. Telling you he didn't know Maura James owned a gun. He wasn't in Blessed over Memorial Day, he was working at the bike shop. All this stuff is just too easy to check. What was he thinking?"

"He was thinking nobody would make the connections. And we almost didn't." Hugh stretches his arms over his head. "Jesus, it's hot in this town. I gotta go home. See my wife and kid."

"It's August, what do you expect?" Kevin says. "And don't think you're leaving me here all by myself with this news conference."

"I don't do well at these things." Hugh sighs. "That psychic from California is a natural. I always come off looking like some bogus cowboy."

Kevin grins. "Ever the optimist. *Lying pimp sheriff from Hicksville,*" he muses. "I think he nailed you."

ALL HALLOWS' EVE

Hᴜɢʜ ᴄʟɪᴍʙꜱ ɪɴᴛᴏ bed with a sigh of relief. Karen is smiling at him.

"How are you tonight, Sheriff?"

"Great. How about you?"

"I'm just fabulous."

"And how is our puppy?"

"Our puppy continues to do his puppy things. Peeing in corners and chewing on end tables. Other than that, he's perfect."

"He'll stop," Hugh says.

"You say." She turns, slipping her arms around him. "How was Halloween?"

"The usual triple A," he says. "Assorted Adolescent Asininity. Biggest thing was a smoke bomb on the courthouse lawn. Making some sort of social statement, no doubt." He kisses her on the neck, gently. "How about sex?" he asks. "Since you're so fabulous?"

Karen yawns. "Thanks anyway. I'm too tired."

"So this is how it works," he says. "You get what you want and then you're no longer interested in sex."

"Don't be such a crybaby. We had fun getting here, didn't we?"

"What did Doc DeVere have to say?"

"Says I'm healthy as a horse, and the due date is June 15. He says my husband is a studly."

Hugh laughs. "Don't overdo it."

"Are you happy, Hugh?" Karen asks. "Tell me the truth."

"I'm happy," he says. "I've got my golden retriever. My wife thinks I'm a studly. What's not to be happy about?"

"Then why the worried look? Did something happen in court today?"

"All good things. The box of stuff Guy Mason collected from the murders—the one we found in his apartment?—was ruled admissible."

"Why wouldn't it be?"

"Defense was trying to get it thrown out on a technicality. But it didn't work."

"When do you testify?"

"Next week. If all goes well."

"Maybe I'll go down there with you. Spend some time with Delia." She raises up on one elbow. "Come on, Hugh. Something's on your mind. What is it? Tell me."

"I keep wondering. What it is that turns an ordinary kid into a killer."

"He isn't an ordinary kid," Karen says. "People who kill that way love killing. Love the depravity of it, the power it gives them." She switches out the light, pressing closer to him. Her body feels warm, comforting next to his. He closes his eyes, but his mind continues to search in the darkness. He wants to *know*. What did Mason really want from those people? Was it anything they had in their power to give him? And does he have it now? Is he satisfied?

The bedside phone rings next to his ear; loud, strident. He snatches up the receiver: "Yeah. DeWitt."

"Hugh, you won't believe this," Ian says. "The Norbois cabin is on fire. I just got a call. It's a big one. Cross Village and Good Hart volunteers are on the way, along with our guys."

"Be right there," Hugh says.

By the time he arrives, two fire trucks are in the driveway, and another is heading up Route 119. Ian's patrol car is parked below the bluff. Above it the fire is roaring; Hugh can hear it from the road. Red-hot cinders hurtle skyward as he climbs the path. Fountains of water are falling through the smoke-filled air. The house is a lost cause, he can see this; the hoses are now concentrating their efforts on the surrounding firs and hemlocks.

"Sarah Clement saw the smoke," Stu Hamilton tells him. "Around three o'clock." Always the good reporter. He is sweating heavily, although the night air is close to freezing. "She was up watching TV. Good thing. Otherwise the whole woods might've gone."

The blaze is so hot, no one can get within a hundred yards of the cabin. The dry woods surrounding it pops and snaps like a load of firecrackers.

The driver of the yellow Link-belt Tractor is waiting on the road. "What a bitch, getting' up that hill!" he shouts. Stu turns to snap a picture of the rig.

"What d'you think?" Ian asks. "Was it kids?"

"Doubt it. Sits empty for four months with paint cans, other flammables in the basement. Nobody keeping an eye on it. Not surprising."

Although Hugh is not certain of that himself. Maybe he wants to believe this once that it's an accident.

"Not to mention the new owners not giving a rat's ass," Ian says.

"Wind's starting to swing north," Stu says.

"Yeah, but Sarah's place is still a quarter of a mile away. They think they'll have it contained in less than an hour. Even ten minutes ago you couldn't stand this close."

"Maybe we got us a firebug," Ian says.

"Don't print that, Stu," Hugh says mildly. "My deputy's restless. He thinks he's underemployed. Missing the excitement."

"He's missing his girlfriend," Stu says.

"What girlfriend?"

Ian doesn't answer. There's a look on his face, as if he's just been caught.

"And don't let him tell you they're just friends," Stu says. "Because that's not what I'm hearing. Ever since she's been down taking that Police Administration course."

"*You and Fredda?*" Hugh asks.

"It's no big deal," Ian mumbles.

"I'm sending her away to school and she's fooling around with my deputy?"

"She said you'd be pissed," Ian says.

"Pissed? Julie Charbonneau's the one who'll be pissed."

Ian grins. "Hey, that was your fantasy, not mine. Anyway, Fredda said you'd say it was unprofessional. That's why she didn't want you to know about it."

"That's okay. I'll just read about it in the *Review.* When are you two planning on getting married?"

"Christmas, probably."

"Oh, Jesus. She's not quitting her job, is she?"

"Don't panic," Ian says. "We'll just be one happy family."

"Hey, I hear the pathologist's report finally came in," Stu says. "So Mason's DNA was in all the female bodies? That and the ballistics report ought to sew it up, right?"

"Ought to. Now his lawyer is pushing the Lost Soul theory. 'Poor kid, no dad to guide him, Mom's a whore, just another fucking victim of circumstance.'"

"They'll keep him until his dick falls off, I hope," Stu says.

"That's the custom," Hugh says. But again he is struck by the precarious nature of things. One can truly count on nothing, know nothing for certain. Yet, it's astounding how hope can carry such weight. When he last saw Valerie Frisch, it was after the news conference announcing Mason's arrest. "I always knew you'd find out the truth," she said. "Rog knew it, too. He just . . . he was in too much pain to wait around. He'd lost hope. You really can't go on without any hope."

He had only planned to stop by, to see how she was doing. She was moving to Minneapolis in order to be closer to her sister and to help take care of her. "And the kids need to get away from here," she said. "They need to remember their father the way they used to know him, not how the newspapers made him out to be. Do you have children yourself, Sheriff DeWitt?"

He told her he did. Then he told her about Petey and how he and Karen had lost him. She listened as he emptied his heart to her. "I think I've lost my hope, too," he said, but she had merely shaken her head. "Oh, I don't think so. I think it's just in hiding. Waiting for you to settle up with your grief." Then she smiled. "There's nothing without meaning in this world, Sheriff DeWitt. Nothing wasted. Rog never wanted to have kids, he was too afraid. He thought they might inherit his illness. But he dearly loved those boys. And now they're my hope. They're my reason to keep going. You'll find your reason, too, I know. Just give it time."

By six-thirty the blaze is under control, and plumes of pungent wood smoke are saturating the early morning air. The charred remains of the cabin rise in shadowy outlines against the faintest of light; the sun won't be up for another hour yet. Hugh watches as the four separate fire departments roll up their hoses. *Hey, Dave! Any of this two-and-a-half yours? Yeah! One section, I think! Those over there are Levering's chains.* Engine No. 2 from Pellston is pulling away down the driveway, and Hugh guides them out. At the side of the road the driver is washing the LS 2700. Amazingly, it is starting to snow.

"Want to grab something to eat?" Ian asks. "Coffee Talk opens at seven."

"I think I'll just go on home," Hugh says.

"Okay, see you later." Ian hesitates. "Don't tell Fredda I told you, okay? About the wedding, I mean."

Hugh grins at him. "You better treat her right, my friend. You'll be answering to me." He heads for the patrol car. Climbing in, he glances upward into a blue velvet sky anchored between the trees; huge white flakes are swirling down like winter leaves, winked away as they're swallowed up by the ashes. A fine mist is in the air; everything silvery, washed in the glow from his headlights. Valerie Frisch had better be right. *Nothing is without meaning. Nothing wasted.* He hopes so. All that one can do is hope.